DON'T
LOOK
BACK

DON'T
LOOK
BACK

DON'T LOOK BACK

JEFF MAGNUSON

...snapped the chip into place and entered the information into the program. He then pressed Enter and placed the headset over his face. As the countdown clock reached "1," and the black screen separated, he could not believe what he was seeing...

Copyright © 2019 Jeff Magnuson
Edited by Jordan Eagles
Cover art and design by Anita B. Carroll, Race-Point.com

This is a work of fiction. Names, characters, businesses, places, events and incidents are either the products of the author's imagination or used in a fictitious manner. Any resemblance to actual persons, living or dead, or actual events is purely coincidental.

First Paperback Edition, April 2019

ISBN 978-0-9990982-6-4

For Dad

DON'T LOOK BACK

I.
Valhalla

1.

July, Present Day

THE RANGE ROVER GLIDED ALONG INTERSTATE 78, SLICING THROUGH THE night fog, when the call came through.

"Yeah?" answered the driver over the speaker phone. The voice on the other end was all business based on her tone and pointed, clear instructions.

"When I tell you to, you are to reset the odometer on your car to zero. From there, you will drive another 3.7 miles exactly, at which time you will see a small road leading off the highway with a metal gate across it. In the middle of the metal gate will be a white and red reflective sign in the shape of a triangle. Approach the sign slowly and turn off your headlights. The gate will open. From there, we will guide you into the facility. Set your odometer to zero in three ... two ... one ... now. You are being watched."

The phone call ended. The driver reset the odometer as instructed and moments later, his car's GPS darkened. The driver, a normally very confident–many would say cocky–man was unnerved by the phone call. The meeting, soon to be taking place, was as important to him as it was to the people with whom he was meeting, but he couldn't help concede that they were the ones calling the shots.

The man was on his way to discuss the latest prototype of a special piece of software commissioned by this private group. Despite working with this group for over two years, and being paid handsomely, he was still very much in the dark about what they planned on using the software for.

The odometer reached 3.6 miles and the driver gradually applied the brakes. Since it was 2:03 a.m., the roads were quiet, and he, therefore, did not look suspicious to anyone as he drove along at thirty miles per hour on the shoulder of the highway. His headlights picked up the reflective sign which was fortunate because the road he was about to turn onto was extremely narrow with overgrown grass on both sides.

The driver stopped his SUV right in front of the gate and waited. After about ten seconds, he received a text message on his phone that simply said, "headlights." The driver turned off his car's headlights and the gate creaked opened. He eased his foot off the brake and the car began its descent into the woods. As his car entered the natural canopy, the driver couldn't see anything. Then, small lights began to illuminate along the edges of the roadway, providing enough guidance for him to slowly navigate his car through the darkness. As his car passed by the lights, they immediately switched off, leaving the paved path he had driven over in complete blackness once again. After about ten minutes, he came to a full stop at a booth where two military types with automatic weapons in their hands were standing guard. The driver's shirt was now sweat-soaked and his anxiety level crept up a notch. *If this is the group's idea of intimidation, it's working brilliantly*, thought the driver.

One of the men approached the driver's side door and stood motionless. The driver rolled down the window halfway and before he could say a word the guard said, "I.D." The driver leaned onto his left side and removed his wallet from his back pocket. He extracted his driver's license from his wallet and fed it to the guard through the open window. The man took the license and instructed the driver to turn off his car and wait. He then went into the booth and sat down at a small desk with a laptop and a scanner on it. The other guard remained motionless at the front gate, continuing to stare directly at the driver.

Three minutes later the guard came out of the booth and whispered something to the other guard who then turned around to open the gate. The guard approached the driver's window again and said, "Mr. Collins, please continue to follow the road through the gate. You may use your headlights at this time, but do not go over ten miles per hour."

Ted Collins was about to ask exactly where the road was going or where to park, but the guard had already returned to his post. He put his driver's license in the cup holder, turned on his car and the headlights, put it in drive, and continued through the gate deeper into the woods.

2.

SAMANTHA MORRISON WAS THE VOICE ON THE OTHER END OF THE LINE. She was also the one authorized to pay Ted Collins and his company over four million dollars for their help with the software he was about to reveal to her. She wore black jeans, black boots, and a black, button down shirt with the first three buttons opened. Her dirty blonde hair was in a tight ponytail, held back with a rubber band. She had a digital jogging watch and was not wearing makeup. She only wore makeup on special occasions because her natural features and uber-healthy lifestyle didn't require its daily assistance. Samantha was twenty-six, single, and pretty much solely focused on her job. She was paid well for her efforts but was also expected to deliver consistent results and keep all issues at bay.

Samantha was waiting at the entrance to the facility with two other armed guards at her side. Valhalla, a research facility, did not look like much from the outside. In fact, it looked like an old, one-level schoolhouse in the middle of the woods. The real nuts and bolts of the facility were underground—six stories down to be precise—all connected by elevators and staircases with a couple of long tunnels leading to emergency panels hidden in the forest floor in case of a needed evacuation.

Ted pulled his SUV around the circular driveway so the passenger window was now only a few feet away from Samantha and a new set of guards. He put the car in park and looked at the three people when Samantha held out her right hand and motioned Ted to come out. He turned off the car, got out, opened the back-rear door, quickly grabbed a black backpack from the backseat, and threw it over his shoulder. He walked around the back of the car, saying a one-second prayer to himself, and then smiled as he extended his arm out to Samantha.

"You must be the person I spoke with, it's nice to—"

"Do you have the prototypes?" said Samantha without acknowledging Ted's attempt at an introduction.

"Yes, I do. They're right here," said Ted as he held up the backpack.

Samantha stared at the backpack in disbelief and said, "You've been carrying around the prototypes in that?"

"Uh, yeah," replied Ted. "What do you expect me to do, put them in a briefcase and handcuff the briefcase to my wrist?"

Samantha shook her head and said, "It would be better than your kid's backpack."

Ted, now starting to lose patience, hastily said, "Look. They're fine. It's the middle of the night. Can we continue this conversation inside?"

"Very well. The guards need to search you and your bag first, then we'll go in."

Ted handed over his bag to one of the guards who took a mini flashlight off his belt, turned it on, and held it in his mouth as he rummaged through the contents of the backpack. There wasn't much other than two black boxes that were the presumed latest prototypes, a booklet, some random, loose paper, and two candy bars. The other guard asked Ted to turn around and extend his arms out so he could frisk him. This was standard procedure, although having him turn around was an old trick that allowed the other guard to remove the candy bars for himself and his partner to eat later. The backpack was then zipped back up and the guard handed the bag back to Ted and nodded at Samantha. Ted was cleared to go with Samantha.

"This way, please," said Samantha, heading toward the steel, front door. She opened the door and motioned for Ted to enter.

"What is this place exactly?"

"You're about to find out," said Samantha as she turned back and nodded at the guards.

3.

Washington, D.C., Three Years Earlier

NICOLAS FOSTER AND HIS LAWYER, DONALD NIMMO, WAITED IN THE conference room. It had been two weeks since the charges were brought against him in a case that the United States Government had been secretly building for close to four years. The news of the indictment and the ten charges levied against him and his company, Sphere, sent the global stock markets into a frenzy. It was the top story on every news station around the world for a full week.

The search engine he built, which played a massive role in how people around the world used the internet, was irresponsibly being used more and more to fatten the pockets of large companies that paid hefty sums for access to the data on consumers around the world. While that in itself was not illegal, there was a much darker side to this entire enterprise.

Through heavily encrypted webpages and back channels, certain people, mostly those who were capable of spending large amounts of money (and who had no shame) could gain access to the personal information of almost anyone. This information included visibility into bank accounts, access to passwords for entertainment subscriptions, and even the ability to listen into private conversations via voice-activated devices that so many people were now using, despite continued reports and complaints of potential spying.

Of course, not everyone was susceptible to this spying. Once again, one could pay the same exact company to block everyone from accessing their personal information. The only issue, aside from the very high cost, was that there was no guarantee that one was really protected.

There were many arguments and discussions within the U.S. Government's offices about how long this could continue to fester before they intervened. To some, it seemed abhorrent that officials could sit idly by as their own citizens were being hacked at alarming rates. Unfortunately, because of the magnitude of the company and its access to the best lawyers, the government had no choice but to build a substantial case over time in order to shut Sphere's operations down for good and send a message to anyone attempting to harm its citizens.

The U.S. Government knew they were getting closer to pulling the trigger on Sphere when they learned about borderline espionage maneuvers taking place. Once there was clear evidence that suggested Sphere was providing data on its own citizens and on smaller government offices to foreign countries, the government knew they had Nicolas Foster right where they wanted him. They also knew that the four years of merely sitting by while other citizens had money stolen and their privacies violated would not have been for nothing.

The door opened and two military police, often referred to as "MPs," entered first. These men were roughly six foot three and close to two-hundred fifty pounds of pure muscle. They also could have been pegged as identical twins, except they weren't even related. They were in their military uniforms and took their places behind Nicolas and his lawyer.

After a minute, the Director of National Intelligence, Jack Burgess, entered the room and sat across from them. He wore a stern expression that seemed to fit his tailored suit and tightly cropped haircut. Jack was in his mid-fifties and had been with the department his entire career after serving honorably in the United States Marines for nearly fifteen years. He was well-respected enough that even the arrogant Nicolas Foster and his lawyer found themselves standing to shake his hand.

"Please, have a seat. We appreciate you coming here," said Jack. Then, looking at the MPs, "Gentlemen? Thank you. We'll need the room." The MPs left the room, closed the door behind them, and waited outside.

"What's this early meeting about exactly?" said Nimmo, immediately pushing aside respect for the man as they got down to business. Donald Nimmo had been practicing for years and had even dealt with the government from time to time, but this request to meet came off as highly unusual and his internal skepticism meter was running hot.

"I'm not going to waste your time or mine," said Jack, looking directly at both men. "As you're aware, the charges against Mr. Foster are significant and, once convicted, would—"

"If convicted, sir," interrupted Nimmo.

Jack stared back silently for a moment and then continued, "Would carry a maximum sentence of life in prison or even death."

"Mr. Burgess, we're well aware of the charges and the potential punishment if convicted. I personally feel that the death penalty is absurd and irrelevant; however, we still have a long way to go with this case."

"We're aware of that fact. The United States has been building this case for four years and we, frankly, do not wish to spend any more time on it."

"Am I hearing that the United States has some type of settlement in mind?" A grin of hopefulness appeared when he said the word "settlement." Jack, ever the master negotiator, noticed this as well as Nicolas's body language as he sat up slightly in his chair. He then knew it was time to lay this out.

"Yes. In a way."

"Well. We're open to hearing what the government would like to offer." Nimmo picked up his pen and twisted it to begin writing on the fresh, yellow pad in front of him.

"What I am about to tell you is highly classified and will, most likely, sound unbelievable to you both. About two years ago, as Mr. Foster's antics were—"

"Alleged antics, Mr. Burgess," Nimmo interrupted again.

Jack sighed. He'd given this guy enough latitude and it was time to reign him in. "Mr. Nimmo. If I so much as hear you breathe heavy, I'm going to have one of the military police, who are right outside that door, escort you out and I will speak with Mr. Foster directly. And yes, I can do that. So, do your client a favor and zip it until I'm through with what I have to say."

Jack stared at Nimmo and then looked over at Nicolas who remained stoic in his seat.

"As I was saying, about two years ago, when we started noticing Mr. Foster's spying tactics reaching criminal levels, someone made a comment during one of our daily briefing meetings about Nicolas and his vast knowledge. It was suggested that he work for the United States to put his snooping expertise to good use for the country that had given him so much. It was an off-hand remark, but myself and a few others started to think about it more seriously. After meeting with the F.B.I. director and the secretary of state several times, we took our idea to the president. We explained the value that Mr. Foster's mind would have in helping us fight a myriad of issues at home and abroad, and not just from a cyber-attack perspective either. Needless to say, he wasn't keen on the idea at first and took several months to mull it over. During that time, we found ourselves having more three-person meetings every two weeks or so which signaled to me at least, that the president was now strongly considering it. As you can probably guess, this project received a green light under the tightest confidentiality about a year ago. Almost immediately, the government commissioned the construction of a facility in western New Jersey on land that is miles from anything, hidden underneath rolling hills and dense pine trees. The location even has restricted airspace above it, similar to many buildings right here in Washington. The general structure existed from years earlier when a wealthy family used the space to privately build and test prototypes of drones and other toys, literally underground. Anyway, the family didn't quite go bankrupt, but close enough, and the facility sat unused for years. We picked it up on the cheap and have poured hundreds of millions of taxpayers' dollars into it to develop our own toys. We have pledged to continue to fund this initiative so long as it produces a benefit to the United States and our allies."

Jack then opened a warm bottle of water that sat in the middle of the conference room table, drank half, and resumed speaking to his now captivated audience.

"The United States wants Mr. Foster to run this facility for us. He will work with me and the other folks mentioned, including the president, in developing and deploying a host of tools that we'll be able to use to combat terrorism and keep our allies and enemies honest. He will need to build out a team, some of whom will most likely be recruited from Sphere. As a reminder, the charges we have against Mr. Foster will also carry over to many of the remaining employees at the company. Then again, maybe they won't. Needless to say, this is a one-time offer and we'll need your decision before you leave here today. If you choose to accept the terms, then we will make the charges brought against Mr. Foster look good to the public by spending the next few months giving the illusion that we are negotiating a plea deal. The deal will end with a judge handing down a sentence of life in prison so the cable news shows, and others, will quickly forget about you. You and your family will be taken care of financially and will have some security protection. Of course, you will also need to move to New Jersey to be near the facility in a home pre-selected for you. Your movements out in public will be practically non-existent, unless you agree to some plastic surgery. But I'm getting ahead of myself."

Nicolas took another sip of water and Nimmo used the brief moment to speak. "And if we decline the government's generous offer?" said Nimmo, his smile now completely gone.

Jack placed the bottle down on the table and folded his hands together in front of him. "Then the United States is going to bring the thunder down on Nicolas and he'll never see anything other than a maximum-security prison for the rest of his life. His wife and daughter will be on their own with whatever money we don't seize combined with whatever Susan can scrape together from a job, if she can even find one. Keep in mind that the Foster name is already tarnished and we'll make sure it's mud when we're done with this case. I don't think I need to remind you of that little issue of espionage that's part of the indictment. What do you think middle America is going to think about a billionaire supporting foreigners with U.S. secrets?"

"That's an exaggeration and you know it," said Nimmo.

Jack laughed slightly. "It's a total exaggeration, but the more times people hear that nonsense, the more they will believe it." Jack shifted in his seat. "Mr. Nimmo, we need Nicolas and we need his colleagues to work for us. This is the best deal they will get. It's either this, doing actual good for their country, or spending the rest of their lives in prison while their families suffer through—"

"We'll take the deal," said Nicolas, speaking for the first time.

"Nicolas, please don't say anything," immediately interjected his lawyer. "We will discuss this in private."

"Then let's discuss. Mr. Burgess, can you please get us the papers. I've heard enough."

Jack looked at Nicolas and then at Nimmo. Nimmo looked back at Jack and simply nodded. Jack then said, "I'll leave you with the paperwork and a lunch menu. You'll want to take a few hours to review. We can talk through a few points, but I have to tell you that most of the points are non-negotiable. I'll check back with you this afternoon. If you need anything, knock on the door and the MPs will assist you."

Jack then stood, buttoned his suit jacket, grabbed his water bottle, walked over to the door, and knocked. One of the MPs opened the door and Jack spoke to him briefly before being handed two thick, bound notebooks. Jack turned and placed the two notebooks on the table, turned back, and walked out of the room.

The MP closed the door leaving Nimmo and Nicolas alone.

4.

Newark, NJ, Six Months Later

THE TELEVISION NEWS VANS EXTENDED ALL THE WAY DOWN THE sidewalk. Some had been in their spots since the previous evening so they could be ready to go live for the morning news shows. Barricades had been erected by the police the afternoon before in anticipation of the mini event scheduled to take place at 10 a.m. As early as 6 a.m., police were starting to divert traffic away from the courthouse and the adjacent streets. As large a headache as this was for the city, and the commuters who would now face morning gridlock, it was necessary as the presence of the most reviled man in America would draw many onlookers.

Nicolas Foster was not the issue—armed U.S. Marshals and city police would make sure of that—rather it was ordinary citizens, some of whom were already camped out behind one of the barricade sections, who had the local police concerned.

Just before 7 a.m., the television spotlights for the on-the-scene reporters glowed as they began to provide the latest update to millions of interested people across the country.

As told by Channel 2's Mary Rivera:

Good Morning. I'm standing outside of the federal courthouse in Newark, New Jersey where a crowd is starting to grow and is expected to be in the thousands. They are all waiting to see Nicolas Foster when he arrives for his sentencing at ten this morning. As you know, he pled guilty back in March to ten counts, including espionage, which carries a potential death

14

sentence. However, as we have already reported, there is little likelihood that this plea deal will include the death penalty. The judge is scheduled to make his announcement this morning, a little over three hours from now.

The buzz continued to build as the morning progressed. The police had set up checkpoints for anyone who wanted to stand on Broad Street, in front of the courthouse. There were a few suspicious items confiscated along with some particularly vulgar, hand-made signs. Generally speaking, the crowd was manageable and did not give the police any real concerns.

The first police motorcycle turned onto Broad Street at 10:01 a.m. followed by four police cruisers, three unmarked, black SUVs, and finally two more police cruisers. As the motorcade slowed down in front of the courthouse, the crowd grew to a deafening roar. People were angry, despite the legal system working in their favor, and they were going to do whatever it took to let Nicolas know about it, personally.

City police officers stood in a line facing the barricade in thirty-foot increments, each armed with a shield and a helmet. As the motorcade came to a full stop, one bystander jumped the barricade causing two of the police to immediately pounce and subdue the threat. The remainder of the crowd continued to yell and a few even hurled small objects at the SUVs.

The police on the motorcycles and in the cruisers exited their vehicles in a formation that was obviously discussed beforehand and, like clockwork, the doors of the three SUVs opened simultaneously. Nicolas Foster was going to be marched directly up the stairs as quickly as possible and,

15

unknown to anyone at the time, this walk would be his very last public appearance.

Various men and women exited the SUVs, wearing sunglasses and dressed in business formal attire with their respective law enforcement medallions hanging around their necks. After surveying the immediate area, one of the U.S. Marshals looked back into the SUV and motioned for Nicolas to appear. As his freshly polished dress shoes hit the pavement, the press, who had a premium spot along and up the stairs, joined in the chorus with their cameras and microphones hoping for a comment, or at least a glance in their direction.

They got neither.

Nicolas put his head down and was flanked on both sides by marshals who each grabbed one of his arms leading him up the stairs. Once inside, there would be no press and no further need for the handcuffs that were pinching his wrists.

The walk lasted twenty-four seconds. Aside from the one jumper, a few items thrown, and a myriad of insults, the event was contained; much to the relief of the law enforcement community.

A low murmur hummed through the courtroom, which was standing room only with members of the public and additional law enforcement. As Nicolas was led into the courtroom, every single pair of eyes turned and stared directly at him. No one made a sound as he was shown to the defendant's seat, next to his lawyer.

The courtroom was not at all like the movies where the ornate wood that encapsulates the cathedral-like ceilings was polished, like in a museum. Instead, the harsh, fluorescent lights reflected back off the white and pinkish, speckled linoleum tiles while the members of the audience sat in cheap, plastic chairs. The seats and tables for the main actors and the jury were wooden, although closer to the assemble-them-yourself kind, than the heavy, darkly stained ones of the past.

"Burn in hell, Nicolas!" a woman shouted from the back of the courtroom. Plain-clothed officers standing nearby immediately escorted the woman out of the courtroom. Screaming like that wasn't a crime but there was a strict, zero-tolerance policy for anyone behaving in a disorderly way anywhere in the courthouse.

Two minutes after Nicolas was seated, the bailiff walked in front of the judge's bench and said in a booming voice, "All rise. New Jersey Federal Court is now in session. Judge Samuel Gait presiding."

Judge Gait walked into the courtroom carrying a manila folder under his arm. He waved his hand for people to sit, as he found the custom of people standing quite annoying, dropped the thick manila folder on the bench, and sat down.

The judge then took his eye glasses out of the case, like he's done for forty years, cleaned the lenses as he looked around the packed courtroom, and placed them on. He then removed several documents from his folder and placed them around him.

"Good Morning. Calling the case of the United States versus Nicolas Foster. Federal case number 23-455466, penalty phase." After another minute, he looked up at the U.S.

Government lawyers and asked, "Mr. Belkin? Anything I need to know before we begin?"

The lawyer rose halfway out of his seat and said, "No, Your Honor." He then sat back down.

The judge looked over at the defense table and continued, "Mr. Foster?"

Nicolas and his lawyer rose out of their seats and Nimmo said, "Not at this time, Your Honor."

"Very well. Please remain standing." Judge Gait adjusted the microphone on his desk, cleared his throat and continued, "Mr. Nicolas Foster. On March first of this year, you pled guilty to ten counts, including a reduced charge of espionage against the United States of America. For the record, this count was reduced because of the relatively small base offense level in addition to multiple gray areas and technicalities regarding who and what was compromised, despite some evidence that suggested the possibility of a larger crime. Furthermore, although the charge of espionage carries a potential sentence of capital punishment, again, unless there is overwhelming evidence to suggest the aforementioned, especially charges to a private citizen, and not a member of the armed services, such a sentence is not appropriate. The remaining nine charges, despite being egregious, dishonorable, and, in some cases, horrific, do not and will not come with the penalty of death."

This last sentence drew several moans from the citizens in the courtroom and another man was quickly escorted out when he made an obscure movement that caught a police officer's attention.

"Order!" shouted Judge Gait from the bench. "I will not be interrupted. If members of this courtroom cannot keep quiet, then you may leave through the doors in the back of the room."

Judge Gait then took a long pause as he slowly looked around the now quiet room. He continued, "Despite the public's wishes, I must do what is just, what is right. Therefore, taking into consideration all of the arguments of both the defense and the prosecution, I have come to the following sentence..."

Members of the press who were seated and standing in the back of the room were huddled over their notebooks getting ready to record the judge's words. While their phones would have made their jobs easier, all electronic devices were strictly forbidden in the courtroom this morning. Additionally, the judge did not allow a live television feed, despite the overwhelming public demand.

"Mr. Nicolas Foster, for the crimes committed over a period of nearly five years for which you have already pled guilty, you are hereby sentenced to life, without the possibility of parole, in the federal supermax prison in Florence, Colorado, effective immediately. This court is adjourned."

Judge Gait rapped his gavel and the courtroom erupted in cheers and chatter as the federal marshals quickly escorted Nicolas into a door adjacent to the Judge's chamber as heading back through the main doors posed too much of a safety risk.

After he was safely inside, several more police officers stood in front of the door. Then, the back doors to the courtroom opened and additional police filed in and began instructing the audience to exit.

Word spread quickly as several reporters immediately ran out when the judge rapped his gavel and made a bee-line to their respective news vans to communicate the news out to the world. Within minutes, all of the news channels had "Breaking News" informing the public of the sentence handed down by Judge Gait.

A few minutes later, an unmarked sedan with blacked out windows along with a patrol car in the front and the rear pulled away from the side of the courthouse on Lafayette Street. This section of the courthouse was completely closed off, and there were four helicopters hovering above. The abbreviated motorcade pulled away at a normal speed so as not to draw attention. They drove to a barricade where officers quickly moved the metal fencing and signaled the cars through. The lead police cruisers had their lights on, but no siren, so the sedan could ease through the four stoplights before making the right onto McCarter Highway which ran through the Ironbound section of Newark and connected with Route 9 leading right into the airport.

The three-car parade crossed onto the airport grounds and followed along the back lanes toward a waiting hangar and, as expected, drew the continued stares of the now five helicopters hovering above.

"We have some time before we can leave. Why don't you both have a seat?" said the lead prosecutor in the case, David Belkin, a baby-faced, ivy-league educated man in his mid-thirties.

Nicolas Foster, Donald Nimmo, two United States Marshals, and David sat in the Judge's annex, a meeting room off to the side of his chambers, normally reserved for larger meetings. The junior prosecutors were busy carrying out their unnamed job requirements of fetching coffee and snacks for everyone from the bakery a few blocks away. The next few hours would be the most important in completing one of the largest government cover-ups of an individual that, so far, had worked out beautifully. Nicolas Foster did commit multiple felonies, but he wasn't going anywhere near Colorado, or a federal prison for that matter. His knowledge and insights were far too valuable to the United States Government to have them rot behind reinforced concrete walls. Instead, he would, ironically, be stationed not too far from the very courthouse where he was just sentenced.

When the Intelligence agencies started getting wind of the depths of the spying that Nicolas orchestrated through the use of the search engine technology that he helped create, they followed very closely. They knew he was going too far with the tracking several years ago, but also saw an opportunity to eventually intervene and utilize it for their own gain. Of course, the idea of essentially black-mailing a citizen to get him to work for the government was outrageous by any decent societal standards, therefore this needed to be handled with the utmost secrecy and care.

The list of people who knew about the operation were few; although that list would begin to grow once Nicolas was brought on board and the facility was properly staffed. Aside from the president, the director of national intelligence, the secretary of state, and the heads of the F.B.I., and C.I.A. currently knew of the cover up. One might say this effort was beyond classified as the implications of this operation getting out would be disastrous on so many levels. The benefits from a national security standpoint, however, were expected to be enormous. The lengths to which Nicolas and his company went to spy on people, places, and events was like nothing the world had ever experienced before. While moles and double-agents existed in almost every country working to secure intelligence, those people also carry a huge risk with them everywhere they go. Aside from potentially being tortured or losing their lives, their families were also at risk along with their own government's secrets, depending on the effectiveness of the persuasion tactics of the enemy. With the amount of knowledge and insights that can now be gleaned from remote locations, agents will eventually be used even less, and true potential threats will be neutralized or foiled before they even have a chance to make a small impact.

Nicolas leaned back in his chair and folded his hands behind his head. "I especially thought the espionage part of the speech was touching. Almost had me convinced I was going away to Yipyap, Wisconsin, or whatever he said."

His smug grin annoyed David, but this whole charade was out of his hands. He was instructed to simply put on a show for the public by memorizing and reciting the talking points that had been provided to him and to remain generally indifferent when in the courtroom.

"Florence, Colorado," replied David. "It's obviously a real place, Nicolas. And, trust me, not one you ever want to visit."

Nicolas waved his hand in a dismissive gesture. "I know. I know. By the way, what did the judge get for this whole thing? Must have been pretty sweet?"

"That's obviously classified." And then, "But, yes, it was substantial."

"Luckiest judge in the world, if you ask me." Nicolas then laughed, snapping both of the marshals out of their daydreams. David ignored the comment and silently counted down the hours until he didn't have to see this guy again.

It wasn't all bad for David, however. In exchange for his lifetime of secrecy and his willingness to execute this dog and pony show, he was paid many multiples of what a typical government prosecutor would make in five years. Everyone sells a little bit of their soul from time to time to help out their family. At least that's what he continues to tell himself when the guilt starts to creep in.

Three hours later, when the coffee and pastries were fully exhausted and the crowds and news vans dispersed, Jack Burgess called Nicolas's lawyer.

"Nimmo," answered Donald.

"Mr. Nimmo? Jack Burgess. We're about ready to move you and Mr. Foster. Instructions will be sent to the marshals. I wanted to give you a head's up so you knew this was official."

"Are we going to the house?"

"Nicolas's wife and daughter are being escorted there now and should arrive within the hour. They'll be at the house when you get there. Just follow the marshals' instructions and, barring any traffic, you'll be in Roseboro by 3 p.m. or so."

"Is there any—"

The line went dead.

Ten minutes later, one of the marshals received a call and stepped out of the room to take it privately. Moments later, he re-entered the room and instructed Nicolas and his lawyer to follow them down a back stairwell. David Belkin was dismissed and left through the courtroom without saying goodbye.

In the underground garage waited one black SUV, similar to the one Nicolas arrived in earlier in the day.

Nicolas looked around and saw no other vehicles and said to the marshal next to him, "Are we really driving out there without an escort?"

"We'll have an escort. The cars are unmarked. One black SUV won't draw stares, but three will. We cannot have anyone be suspicious, even in middle-of-nowhere New Jersey. Step in, gentlemen."

Nicolas and his lawyer did as they were told and the two marshals got in the front and passenger seats. Once the garage door opened, they slowly drove up the ramp to the sidewalk where they waited for the lead car to drive past. After about thirty seconds, a red Jeep Grand Cherokee passed them and the marshal hit the gas to follow directly behind it. Behind them, were two more cars but Nicolas had no idea which ones were the escorts as the cars that piled behind them all looked like regular people going about their day.

What none of them noticed, at least not right then, was the white Hyundai Sonata with two men inside, about four cars back, eyeing the black SUV.

On the trip to Roseboro, there would be no sirens and no speeding. Additionally, the government's paranoia about transporting Nicolas also eliminated the idea of taking a helicopter since those flights would need to be officially logged and could therefore potentially be traced. In this case, they were a happy family of four on their way to a mansion in Roseboro so a criminal could officially begin his second life as a spy for the United States and potentially have even more power than he had at the company he built.

The unmarked third motorcade of the day merged onto Interstate 78 near Newark Airport just as the decoy private plane, stationed in the hanger at the airport from hours earlier, began to pull out. A fresh batch of helicopters hovered over the scene catching Nimmo's attention but not arising any alarm as the choppers were clearly not moving to follow the car he was currently in.

What makes I-78 especially interesting in New Jersey is the contrast of views and neighborhoods when starting at the very beginning and traveling through the state. Heading west, the familiar views that anyone who has flown into Newark Airport would quickly recognize—the cities of Newark, Elizabeth, and Irvington, the seaport with tons of cargo containers stacked up, refineries belching smoke, and IKEA—soon disappear and are replaced with lush, green trees that line the highway on both sides. Upscale towns like Summit and Bedminster are hidden behind those trees and have a range of homes from modest and comfortable to truly outrageous pieces of property. Farther on, about ten miles past the intersection of I-287, the state becomes more rural. Here there are quieter towns, farmland, and a lot more plots of rolling hills; essentially the exact opposite of what one would have seen out of a car window thirty minutes earlier. And it is at the beginning of the farmland stretch where the black SUV is with its unmarked escorts and the white Sonata that has remained a steady three cars behind.

The two people in the Sonata were clearly not experienced at tailing cars as they had already tipped their hand to the two marshals sitting in the front seat of the SUV. For one, they had not budged from their third position since they merged onto the highway. In a normal traffic pattern, cars jockey back and forth and rarely stay behind the same vehicle for very long. The SUV was locked in at the sixty-five mile per hour speed limit, coasting along in the right lane. On more than one occasion, the marshal in the passenger seat noticed the passenger in the Sonata raise a camera and point it at them. What their camera would not be able to pick up were the rearview cameras mounted high on the back liftgate of the SUV. Those live images were being transmitted to both the marshal, who was monitoring the images on his phone, and to an undisclosed, remote location where this entire trip was being closely watched.

Neither Nicolas nor his lawyer had any idea of the situation brewing. That was by design. It wasn't their issue. It was the marshals' and the government's issue and plans were already in motion to correct this disturbance.

One minute later, as the marshal in the passenger seat was about to call in the Sonata, his phone vibrated. He unclipped his phone from his belt, held it up to his ear, and said, "Yeah?"

He listened without making a sound and then finally said, "Got it," and hung up the phone. He re-clipped his phone onto his belt and looked over at his colleague driving the SUV and said, "White Sonata. Three cars back. Eighty-five in ten seconds. Left lane."

The driver glanced into the rearview mirror and then looked into his sideview mirror and stepped on the gas. He didn't force it up to eighty-five as that would have been a dead giveaway. Instead, he gradually accelerated and moved them into the left lane. Sure enough, the white Sonata followed suit and began regaining the distance it had lost. After about a minute, the Sonata now sat two cars back from the SUV with one of the unmarked escorts separating them. When the driver glanced back, the red Grand Cherokee had pulled alongside the Sonata in the middle lane. The escort in front of the Sonata hit the brakes hard, causing the driver of the Sonata to hit the brakes, skid, and instinctively swerve to his left since his right side was blocked. The Sonata quickly found itself on the shoulder and then the median, a grass depressed ditch that separated the east-bound land from the west-bound lane, bouncing along the uneven terrain, drawing stares from cars on both sides of the highway, until it came to a full stop. The marshal's phone then rang once again.

"Yeah." And then, "Got it." Without even looking at the driver this time, "Right lane. Resume speed."

"Got it."

The motorcade continued on, deeper into rural New Jersey.

At 3:15 p.m. the black SUV pulled up the winding driveway in Roseboro where two other unmarked cars were parked. These cars transported Nicolas's wife, Susan, and daughter, Abby, earlier in the day. Nicolas emerged from the car and stretched his arms high in the air like a free man even though his every move would be monitored by the government from now on. He didn't care. He had already bought into the fact that the work he would be doing would be critically important for national security for the foreseeable future. Susan, on the other hand, had been a tougher sell on this new lifestyle, even though the alternative of living on whatever the government agreed to let her keep along with the fact that her husband would not be around would be a nightmare. By now though, she had come to realize that they were all being given the enormous gift of a second chance, and her focus was to make a normal life for Abby in western New Jersey.

The house and the property were big. Much bigger than Nicolas thought even though he was able to see pictures and drone footage a couple of months ago. Susan designed the whole house using virtual tours and photos as neither she nor Nicolas were allowed to visit the property until today, the official move-in date. Nicolas looked around and quickly realized that he could not see another house or hear anything, other than birds chirping. He was totally isolated. Even though he couldn't see all of it, a fence surrounded the entire perimeter of the property and had motion sensors on every other main post that allowed for full coverage of the fence line including six feet out on either side. While natural animals would certainly trigger the sensors, the system was smart enough to adjust to natural movements of hundreds of different species of animals and would only trigger if there was unnatural movement, such as a human attempting to scale the vertical iron bars.

"This way, gentlemen," said one of the agents emerging from the garage.

Nicolas and Nimmo followed into the garage and then into the house's mudroom. From there, they made their way into the large living room with its fifteen-foot vaulted ceiling and enormous sectional couch.

"Daddy!" said Abby as she ran into her father's arms.

"How's my sweetie?" said Nicolas, carrying his three-year old and displaying a softer side that none of the agents had seen in the last several months. "You like your new home, Abby?"

"Yeah! It's so big!"

"It sure is. We're gonna have a good time here, right?"

"Yes," she said, nodding her head.

Nicolas smiled as he put his daughter down and kissed Susan hello.

"You okay?" asked Susan.

"Fine. Easy trip. How are you?"

"Tired."

"Yes," said Nicolas through a sigh. "Definitely tired." Nicolas hugged his wife and then looked at the other people still in his living room. The Deputy Director of National Intelligence, Jack Burgess's number two, Wanda Platts, stepped forward.

"Mr. Foster, I'm sorry but we need to speak with you for just a few more minutes before we leave."

Susan rolled her eyes. "Seriously? Can't you let us get sett—"

"Honey," interrupted Nicolas. "It's okay. This will just take a second. It's almost over."

Nicolas went to kiss Susan's forehead again, but she moved away too quickly.

"Come on Abby. Let's go up to your room while your father says goodbye," said Susan.

Abby took her mother's hand and they walked out into the entrance hallway and up the stairs.

Nicolas waited until they were upstairs and then looked back at Wanda and said, "Any chance we can make this quick? I really don't need our first night here to be a fight."

"We don't want to take up any more time but we must discuss a few points," said Wanda.

"Well," said Nicolas looking around, "Have a seat. I'd offer you all something but I don't even know what my kitchen looks like, much less where anything is."

"We're fine, thank you." They all took a seat in the living room.

"What was that issue with the car back on the highway? That was a pretty slick move by the escorts."

"We believe they were photographers for some tabloid magazine. They were unharmed but they also earned themselves the eyes and ears of the government for the foreseeable future. We cannot let them get anywhere near here. We don't think they will but if they try, they'll certainly regret it. Now, in two days we'll take you over to the facility to give you a tour but, before we do that, we need to discuss how you are going to start to build it out from a personnel perspective.

"We need to do this now?" said Nicolas.

"Not every employee, but a main one, yes. The government is getting ready to bring indictments on several former employees of yours and, well, you saw how long it took to sort out your deal. We expect deals with lower level employees to move much faster and we want you involved in speaking with them about what we are going to be doing here."

"To encourage them?"

"Exactly."

"How many am I allowed?"

"That's still being worked out, but what we need from you right now is who will be your immediate replacement should something happen to you."

Nimmo immediately chimed in, "That sounds pretty ominous, Ms. Platts. Are there already more threats against my client? No one knows he's here," said Nimmo.

"No new threats, but we must have precautions starting now. The work that we'll be doing cannot only be known by one individual at the facility," said Wanda.

"I'm assuming Samantha Morrison is on your hit list?" said Nicolas, looking at his house guests.

"At the very top."

"She's the only one for the job as far as I'm concerned. The others could potentially fill smaller roles, if necessary, but I trust Samantha like I trust my wife."

"You're firm on this, Nicolas? There's no going back."

"One-hundred percent. Frankly, she'd probably run the place better than me except her technical knowledge isn't quite at the same level as mine."

Wanda's aide, Christoph scribbled something into his notebook. "She's only twenty-three years old."

"And?"

Christoph glanced at the others and then Wanda spoke again, "Well, we appreciate your honesty. Now, before I go, there is one more thing I have to say to you in the presence of your lawyer."

Nicolas looked at his lawyer who simply nodded back at him.

"As of right now, everything you do in life will be monitored. This includes phone calls, trips to the store, which, you are forbidden to take for at least a year, and all other movement. You will be driven to and from the facility every day. You are not permitted behind the wheel of any vehicle, which is part of the reason why you will not receive a driver's license. We do not have visual access to anything in your home. Even in this extreme situation, we have standards and respect your family's right to privacy." Wanda couldn't help offer that last snarky dig at Nicolas.

"Thanks," said Nicolas.

"If you attempt to compromise anything about Operation Ghost, including people in the operation, I have the authority and the president's blessing to terminate you. Do you understand?"

Nicolas's eyebrows raised. "Ah, so this was the missing clause from the ninety-page agreement?"

"That's correct," said Wanda. "Your lawyer has been made aware of this in private discussions to which he, presumably, has already informed you."

Nicolas just smiled.

"Do you understand this Nicolas?"

Nicolas stared past the deputy director for a few moments while rubbing his hands together when he said, "I understand. I just have two things."

"What's that?"

"Who came up with Operation Ghost?"

"I did. Why?"

"Because it's idiotic, that's why."

Wanda sighed and turned up her hands. "Do you have a better suggestion?"

"Yes," said Nicolas, smiling. "Valhalla. Not Operation Valhalla. Not Top-Secret Valhalla. Just Valhalla. That's the new name of the facility and the on-going operation."

Wanda stifled a chuckle, finding Nicolas's insistence on the name of an organization that few will ever know about to be a little absurd and childish. She then said, "What was the other thing?"

"Take your men and get the hell out of my house."

Wanda stared at Nicolas, not surprised by his reaction, nodded at Nimmo, stood, along with the others, and walked back out through the mudroom and into the garage. A few moments later the three cars started up and headed back down the driveway and out toward the highway.

As they drove back along the highway, Wanda took out her phone and looked up what Valhalla was. She knew the name from various cities around the world but figured that's not what Nicolas was referring to. She came across what she suspected was the answer which read in part:

A mythological, vast hall. A god chose certain warriors who died nobly in battle to travel to Valhalla...

Wanda clicked off her phone and shook her head. Despite essentially given a second chance at life, *Nicolas certainly still has not learned any humility,* she thought to herself.

"Valhalla," Wanda muttered.

"I'm sorry?" said Christoph, glancing in the rearview mirror.

"Nothing. It's just ... nothing."

5.

Valhalla, July

SAMANTHA AND TED PROCEEDED THROUGH THE MAIN DOOR—WHICH WAS a reinforced steel plate weighing close to one ton—and just as the door closed, Ted saw an enormous deadbolt automatically slide across the door and into the wall. A computer panel that rested on the wall had a series of lights that changed from green to red, signaling the alarm was now activated. He turned back as dim lights slowly illuminated the dark space. Samantha continued to walk forward and pressed a button on the wall causing hidden elevator doors to open. They both stepped in and Samantha placed her right thumb on an angled piece of glass that jutted out from the wall. A green light appeared, the door closed, and the elevator descended.

"Tight security," offered Ted a bit nervously.

"It has to be. In fact, that small hallway we were just in is all that upper part is. The rest of the space within the upper structure are various wires and motion detectors for added security."

"Seems excessive," said Ted looking up.

A small smile formed on Samantha's lips.

The elevator came to a stop and the doors opened. The lighting in this new room was a little brighter as they came upon another two guards, both female, seated behind a desk looking at various flat screens.

"I guess we need to check in at reception," snarked Ted.

Samantha stopped and grabbed his arm, preventing him from walking any farther.

"Mr. Collins, I suggest you immediately lose whatever sass and charm you think you are attempting. Either of these women could snap your neck within five seconds if I asked them to. They are both highly trained officers and happen to also oversee the other guards you've already met this evening. In other words, be polite."

The smile disappeared from Ted's face and he curtly responded, "Yes, ma'am." He was glad no one from Collins Industries was there to see this treatment.

"That's better," said Samantha. "Now, just stand right there for a second."

Samantha walked over to the desk and both women rose to their feet. Ted could not hear what they were saying, and he wasn't about to appear nosy either, so he just stared at his feet.

After a few moments, Samantha turned around and motioned for Ted to come to the desk.

One of the guards held up a mini camera no bigger than an earbud and said, "Look right here, sir."

Ted did as he was told and the guard captured his digital image. She then sat back down and typed a few commands into her computer. Ten seconds later a door on the right popped open and the guard looked at them both and said in an expressionless tone, "You may go in now."

"Thank you," said Samantha. Then, turning back to Ted who was looking around the room, "Mr. Collins, what you are about to see, you cannot unsee, do you understand?"

"I understand," said Ted.

"Good. And since you cannot unsee it, you will remember this place for a long time. Everything beyond this door is highly confidential. It is rare, and I mean rare, that civilians are allowed on these premises at all. However, given the work that you and your company are doing, you also have skin in the game, so we're allowing this meeting to take place at this secure location. You've heard this before, but you are not, I repeat, not to speak of what you are about to see to anyone. Ever. The consequences of you doing so would be dire. Is that understood?"

"Yes, I understand."

"Good. Welcome to Valhalla, Mr. Collins. This way please."

Samantha led Ted through the doorway into the first laboratory.

*

The only laboratory that Ted knew like the back of his hand was the Research & Development lab at his company's headquarters in Oak Brook, New Jersey. He thought *that* was impressive considering what they have been able to develop over the years. Additionally, he'd been in facilities where aviation enhancements were worked on for both commercial airplanes and military jets, and while the scale of those labs was enormous, he was never really "wowed" by them.

The room he was standing in now, though, caused his mouth to open in awe, if ever so slightly and undetected. The ceilings were cavernous, at least five stories high, with catwalks crisscrossing overhead and several cubicle-like work spaces with up to six flat-screen monitors in each station all throughout the lab floor. Additionally, there were empty rooms surrounding the perimeter with glass walls on three sides of each room, which struck Ted as a little bizarre.

"Are those conference rooms?" said Ted, pointing at a row of rooms that lined the far wall.

"Those are testing rooms, actually," said Samantha. "We're always working on various prototypes here and we need the space to test as we cannot go outside. The glass walls on the sides of each room actually slide so the space can become one giant room."

"I see," said Ted, taking mental notes and thinking of all the ways to apply this design aesthetic to Collins Industries.

They continued slowly through the first lab, which had many more people working than Ted would have expected at this hour of the night. Ted imagined that the space was chock full during regular hours with people running around frantically. *Maybe I'll ask about that later*, he thought to himself.

As they were walking around, Ted looked up at a giant thirty-foot screen that seemed to be part of the natural wall—the centerpiece of the room. The video images kept changing every five seconds and before Ted could even ask, Samantha chimed in, "Satellite images from all around the world. We are the only ones with the capability to zoom in to this degree and still have a clear image. Obviously, I cannot tell you what these are images of ... and you probably wouldn't want to know anyway."

Ted couldn't take his eyes off the screen. "It's amazing. Almost like we're right there, looking down from a rooftop." Out of the corner of his eye, he then saw two birds flying overhead. "What the hell?" said Ted, flinching, the birds breaking his concentration.

"Ah," said Samantha, now looking up. "You're lucky. You're here at the right time. We can only test these birds off hours."

Ted was confused. "What exactly do you mean by 'test the birds?' I really don't need, or want, to see any animal testing."

Samantha smiled. "Mr. Collins, those are not real birds. They were built right here in this lab. Actually, they technically were built in Lab #2, one level down, but since this is the biggest room in the facility, it's also used as a testing ground."

Ted, staring at what he had thought were two normal birds a few seconds ago, stammered, "Maybe I'm a little slow. They're not real? They're flying like normal birds."

Samantha smiled again; she seemed to be enjoying this. "You're correct. It has taken us three years to get to this point.

In fact, these house sparrows are one of the first projects we started developing when this facility was opened. They are cameras, controlled by a remote system operated right here in Valhalla. There are ten cameras built inside what, to the human eye, looks like a real sparrow. The idea is that no one will ever notice or pay close attention to them. Since these birds are so ordinary, there is very little risk of them being shot at by hunters or anyone else for that matter. No one really pays them any mind."

"What about kids with BB guns?" said Ted, immediately regretting his idiotic remark.

The smile quickly faded from Samantha's face. "This way please," she said and walked on.

"Hang on a sec," said Ted, running to catch up to Samantha. "Sorry, my mind is just blown by this. What will be they used for?"

"That I cannot say, Mr. Collins, but let's just leave it at whatever you think they can be used for, probably won't be too far off the mark. There's only so much law enforcement a town or city can manage and, frankly, the extra help is usually welcomed."

"But I don't understand. How will you be able to keep this a secret? Even if regular folks never realize that these things are not real birds, surely this will get out somehow."

Samantha's gaze turned steely and she took a step toward Ted.

"I told you that what you will see here cannot be unseen. We have a list of everyone who knows what we are doing here. It's not a very long list, and now your name, Ted Collins, is at the bottom of it. If word does get out about anything that goes on here, Mr. Collins, we have the means to quickly find out who leaked the information. Understand?"

Ted smiled. "Yep. Got it."

Samantha continued to stare at Ted, unconvinced that he was fully grasping the gravity of her statement. "Just to be sure you've really got it, let me tell you a quick story about someone who also said he 'Got it' once and what happened to him.

"About two years ago, we commissioned a contractor, let's call him Syd, to install some solar paneling that we needed for some projects we were working on. He was carefully vetted and cautioned about the level of secrecy that was required. He worked here for about two months, the project was completed, and he left. On his last day, he was, again, warned about saying anything. Well, needless to say, he started blabbing to his friends, even posting a blurry picture of the work he completed online, which earned him a visit from myself and a few others to remind him again. This time he was rude and condescending, threatening to get a lawyer, blah, blah, blah and vowed that it was his right to speak of Valhalla if he so chose. The next day, we paid him another visit and let's just say he hasn't been heard from since. By anyone."

Ted was frozen. Then, after a moment, said somberly, "I actually remember the story of the guy disappearing. It seemed bizarre, especially for this area. They never found him, if I recall," said Ted.

Samantha stared back at Ted. "See what I mean, Mr. Collins? Do you get it now? This way please."

"I have to ask. What about his family? He had little kids."

"Reparations were made." Samantha continued walking.

Ted continued to follow Samantha and became more and more uncomfortable the deeper they ventured into the facility. Samantha arrived at another set of doors at the far end and placed her finger on a glass plate, similar to the elevator, and the door opened.

Samantha turned toward Ted and said, "We're going into a conference room now where you can present us with the latest developments. There will be three other people in the room and we will video record the session so additional people can be briefed in the morning."

"How much time do I have to present?" asked Ted nervously, feeling like he was a student again, having to present in front of the class. Contrary to his confidence as an adult, as a kid he would often feel physically ill when he had to do any form of public speaking, no matter how small the crowd.

"As much time as you need. We're expecting to hear good progress."

Samantha and Ted walked through the door, down another hallway, and into a conference room.

As they entered the room, there were several things Ted noticed right away. First, the room was dimly lit, making the three other people in the room hard to see. Second, along the backwall was a mirror that Ted assumed (correctly) was a one-way mirror with an unknown number of people seated on the other side of the glass. Samantha motioned for Ted to stand in the front of the room. The lights on the ceiling were then turned on, angling down in his direction. These lights did not give Ted's eyes the chance to adjust to see who else was in the room, which was very unsettling. He was starting to feel queasy, flashbacks of the past.

"Mr. Collins, for security purposes I cannot introduce you to nor let you see the other people in this room," said Samantha, taking a seat at the far end of the table with the other members.

"Okay. Do you want me to—"

Two armed guards, the same guards who searched Ted twenty-five minutes prior, entered the room and closed the door behind them. One walked around to the other side of the table while the other guard stayed right by the door.

Silence filled the room as Ted placed his backpack on the table.

"Mr. Collins. How many prototypes are in your bag?"

Ted began unzipping the bag. "Unless these two guys took them out along with my candy bars, there are two," said Ted, looking at both guards.

"We'll reimburse you for the candy bars, Mr. Collins. For now, please remove the prototypes and whatever else you have for us and place them on the table."

Ted, looking at Samantha despite no longer being able to see her because of the lights, opened his bag. His eyes were beginning to water and he started to perspire from the lack of air flow in the room. He placed the items on the table and Samantha motioned to the guard at the other side of the table, who immediately walked over, grabbed the items, and walked them to the back of the room. The manual was quickly skimmed by another hidden colleague. Samantha personally inspected the prototypes that sat snug in an indentation inside the black boxes. Both prototypes were identical: red, circular chips, about the size of a nickel with a small design etched on the top.

"Ted, what's this design?" said Samantha.

"Just a little something we came up with. Most of our chips just have a number on them. We wanted to play around with an actual design."

"I see. Can you explain to me what it means?"

Ted thought it was pretty obvious but took the bait anyway. "We thought the two counter-clockwise arrows were a good icon for the Look-Back feature. That's what we've been calling it. We didn't spend too much time discussing it. I think one of the techs came up with it in passing and we just stamped all the chips with it."

Samantha raised her head and looked Ted straight in the eye. "So, just to be crystal clear, these latest prototypes also fit directly into the Phase I headsets, Mr. Collins?"

"They do," replied Ted. "You still have those, I assume? I didn't bring any extra with me."

"We have six or so." Samantha then whispered something to the group around her and then to the guard who was still at the far end of the table with her. After a few moments, both guards approached Ted and stood on either side of him.

"What's going on?" said Ted.

"There will be nothing further, Mr. Collins," said Samantha. "Our team is going to inspect these prototypes and we'll move forward internally. You can thank your team for their great work. The remaining balance of the four-million-dollar fee will be wired to you once we are satisfied with what you have brought us."

"But they're not done yet," said Ted, nervously. "I'll need those prototypes to make any additional changes."

"No additional changes will be necessary. We will take it from here," said Samantha. Then, nodding at the guards, "Gentlemen, show Mr. Collins out."

The guards moved closer to Ted. As they were approaching, the conference room door swiftly opened and the two female "receptionists," with stun batons now hanging from their hips, came into the room and stared directly at Ted.

He grabbed his bag and, again, looked in Samantha's direction saying, "How do I know you won't stiff me on the balance of what's owed?"

"Because we honor our commitments and expect anyone who does business with us to honor his. You'll get your money, however, not until we test them out ourselves. Our plan is to begin working on these tomorrow. We now have the proper personnel to manipulate and refine this technology—along with producing any new ones we may need. Your work has taught us a lot over the years.

"At this point, you'll need to destroy any additional Red Chips and manuals that you may have in your possession. As you'll recall, part of the contract is for us to conduct random inspections to ensure that neither you nor your company is benefitting in any way from any, shall we say, misplaced or forgotten prototypes. We expect you to honor this deal as we have. Additionally, any employees or associates of yours who do not comply with the terms will be *your* responsibility. Let me remind you again of poor Syd and his family, Mr. Collins."

Ted paused, aware that he had no leverage in this room.

"You have what we produced," he muttered. "There's nothing else."

"Good. The guards will show you back to your car now."

Samantha and the others sat silently as they watched Ted follow the guards out of the room. After the door shut, a voice from behind the glass filled the conference room.

"Was the Syd story really necessary, Samantha?" said the voice.

Samantha looked back at the glass and said, "It was. His attitude while we were walking though the facility was a little too cavalier for my taste. I didn't go into any sort of detail. He may have a lot of money and a big company that his daddy handed to him, but he's not too bright. We can pretty much tell him anything."

The exit route out of the lab was different from the way he came in. Instead of going back through the main floor with the giant screen, the guards led Ted down the hallway in the other direction until they came to another elevator. They got on and, just like before, the guard used his thumbprint to activate the door. The elevator ascended to Level -1 where all three men got off. The long hallway they were now in was almost completely pitch black, except for a few pin lights every ten feet or so along the edges of the floor. Ted couldn't help but notice the similarity between the lighting here and the road he came in on.

Despite the low visibility, the men walked quickly in silence until they reached the end of the hallway. The doors opened after one of the guards pushed an illuminated green button on the wall. Beyond the doors was a staircase and the men climbed up, turned around at the first landing, and completed the climb to Level 0. A guard opened the door and all three men were now back in the entrance to the building. Ted, having his bearings back in place, relaxed a little.

The alarm panel switched from red to green and the guard said, "Sir, please exit through that door. The guards out front will escort you to the gate."

Ted watched as the two guards went back through the doors and back down the staircase. Ted looked around the main entrance one last time, shook his head in disbelief, and exited the building.

The road out of the Valhalla facility was slightly different as well. Fortunately for Ted, his GPS resumed working once he was escorted through the gate, which was another hidden, unassuming road that led onto a quiet backroad. Ted was unsettled at what had transpired at the end of the meeting. Thoughts raced around his head as his SUV headed back along the same stretch of highway he had driven in on.

6.

Saturday, October 28, Three Months Later

IN THE WEE HOURS OF SATURDAY MORNING, THREE PEOPLE, INCLUDING Ted, were seated around a small table in the corner of Ted's office. Ted had just finished debriefing his closest colleagues, Roy Walker, head of Research & Development, and Jane Stafford, Collins' number two, about what took place a few months ago with Samantha at Valhalla. Of course, the story he told them was a much different tale than what *really* happened—he wasn't about to divulge how she embarrassed him and then threw him out of the facility—but it was enough for them to get the idea. The two confidants seated around the table were stunned at what they were hearing. Both Jane and Roy had no idea that they had been developing the Red Chip technology for private use and felt betrayed by this information. They also knew that this meeting was not intended for Ted to have a forum in which to air his grievances. These two had worked for Ted since he took over Collins Industries ten years ago, and they waited to hear what his plan was.

Ted always had a plan.

Ted leaned forward, interlocked his fingers on the table, and said, "I've decided that we're going to introduce the Red Chips to the general public anyway, but we'll modify the technology slightly so as to appear different from what this group now has."

Silence hung in the office like the remaining fog outside.

Ted took a sip of his convenience store coffee and unwrapped a black and white cupcake from its cellophane wrapper. Before biting off half, he looked around at his two colleagues, somewhat bothered that no one had spoken yet, and asked sarcastically, "So, does anyone have any questions?"

"Yeah, I do," said Roy, snapping out of deep thought. "We only have three more Red Chips in our possession, and further testing needs to be done as well as significant enhancements. They're not ready for the public yet, not even close. If I had known about this new timeline, I could have been working to produce more."

"I do realize that, Roy," said Ted, taking another sip of his coffee to wash down the cupcake. "How much time is needed to get these chips to where we can initially roll them out? Say two-hundred and fifty of them?"

Roy stared right over the top of Ted's partially bald head and thought to himself before saying out loud, "Best guess? Six months to a year."

"Probably more than that," chimed in Jane. "We're going to need to clear this technology across the appropriate channels first. This isn't just a new video game, Ted. These Red Chips can, and will, have significant implications if used incorrectly or if they fall into the wrong hands."

"Let me worry about that, Jane," said Ted, putting up his hand dismissively. "This group is not the only one who gets to call the shots. There's really no telling what they'll do with the technology now that they have it, including selling it to our competitors for much more than they paid for it. My only regret is not saying 'no' to them when they first asked. I should have used the idea to develop it for ourselves only. That would have been the smarter move."

"We thought that's what we were doing all along," said Roy, somewhat dejected.

"I know," said Ted in a reassuring tone. "Don't worry. All of this work is not going to go to waste."

"And what is this private group? What are they going to use the Look-Back technology specifically for?" asked Jane.

"The less I say about this group, the better for you both. Trust me there. And, I have no idea. They wouldn't say." Ted then tried to diffuse the situation by stating, "Also, our lawyers have informed me that the Agreement we signed years ago does not hold us or this company liable in any way."

Jane nodded in a weak agreement, keeping her heavy skepticism and the rest of her questions to herself.

Roy spoke up again, "Ted, if we can agree that we'll test a few of these discreetly in a small market first, then we can hit six months. Is that reasonable?"

"It is. In fact, I want to bring this up at our executive meeting in a few months."

Jane immediately spoke again, "Ted, forgive me, but I don't think that's a good idea. The more people who find out about this, the more risk we have. You just said so yourself."

Ted anticipated this push-back and replied, "Let's not get ahead of ourselves. The Red Chips are not going anywhere near the public just yet. People need to first become aware of the Phase I virtual reality headsets which we haven't even formally rolled out yet and, by the way, are great pieces of work just by themselves."

Jane and Roy remained resigned as Ted's compliment flew right over their heads.

"My plan is to test just the new headsets with the public starting today." Ted was still receiving hesitation from his colleagues to which he finally offered, "We have done, and continue to do, amazing work in this company. And I'm not just talking about the new hologram TVs and smart phone batteries that last for a week, which are game changers in their own right." Ted paused for effect. "That little Red Chip could make this company, especially this group sitting right here, one of the most critical and important players in the world. And that's not an exaggeration."

They sat in silence for a few moments; Roy and Jane staring out the window, Ted finishing his cupcake. Roy then stepped out to use the bathroom (and to take a few deep breaths).

About five minutes later, Steve Lewis knocked on the door frame of the office and Ted jumped up to greet his old friend. Ted and Steve grew up and went to high school together in the late 1980's. Ted was very much the stereotypical football playing jock with a known bullying streak. Steve, on the other hand, was closer to the nerd-end of the high school spectrum and, fortunately for him, was not only spared from Ted's nonsense, but actually embraced by him. By good fortune, they grew up near each other and their parents were close friends which, by default, meant that their kids would be required to get along. They took different paths for college but both managed to gravitate back home to Oak Brook. In the present day, Ted now owned a mammoth technology company and

Steve was the manager of the electronics department at Southfield's, a department store connected to a shopping mall in the middle of town. Over the years, Ted had not once offered Steve an opportunity to work for him at Collins Industries for which Steve was both resentful and relieved. To Steve, the idea of dealing with Ted on a daily basis as adults was so unappealing that even the lure of a higher salary and a more respectable job title didn't matter. And yet, as bad luck would have it, Ted's close relationship with the owner of the mall property allowed him to routinely test out his new products locally at Southfield's. So, despite his best efforts, Steve was now indirectly working for Ted and receiving nothing in return for his services.

"Morning everyone," said a surprisingly upbeat Steve, pulling up a chair. "Kinda early for a meeting, no?"

Jane and Roy smiled. Ted sat back down and handed Steve a Phase I headset.

Steve inspected the item and said, "Nice. Upgrade from the earlier ones I take it?"

"Exactly right," said Ted. "We've expanded the database of locations and the visual effects and graphics are substantially sharper."

Steve continued to inspect the headset and, sure enough, his eagle eye caught the little slit on the left side.

"This slit here. Does this open?"

Roy shifted slightly in his seat which Steve caught out of the corner of his eye.

Ted smiled. "All in time, my friend. A shipment of headsets will be arriving at your store later today. We want to push these headsets pretty aggressively as we need to be sure they are working properly and that the people love 'em."

"Okay, but if you're not going to tell me about all of the features, how can you expect me to sell these on the floor?"

"The Red Chip is not ready to make its debut just yet," said Ted, immediately regretting opening his big mouth. Jane quietly seethed.

"What Red Chip?" said Steve, looking over at Jane. He then lowered the headset and looked at Ted. "Ted, why am I here at 7 a.m. on a Saturday?"

Ted waved his hand in front of face. "It's nothing. Forget it. It's a future enhancement that's still being worked on. You're here, my friend, because we need you to push these headsets hard. We need to understand what people think of them before we roll out the enhancement."

"Have you considered the few customers who will notice this compartment and then inquire?"

"Yes, we have. First, as you already saw, this panel is actually hard to see for most people, and even harder to open, all by design, so it acts as a natural deterrent. If anyone does inquire about the panel, our customer service team has been told to simply say it's part of the design. Finally, there's no mention of the Red Chip anywhere that the public can see and there's a zero percent chance that anyone will be able to manipulate the headset."

Steve shrugged. Those issues were not his problem. He just liked to push Ted's buttons when the opportunity presented itself. "If you say so. What time can we expect these?"

"I'd say around ten-thirty or so," said Ted. Then looking around at the other two before taking another sip of his coffee, "Everyone good?"

Ted received three blank stares.

7.

Pete

sen·ior·i·tis (*sēnyə'rīdəs*) – a condition where seniors in high school stop caring about school completely. This typically occurs during the spring semester when the prospect of leaving high school forever starts to sink in.

PETE DAVIS HAS SENIORITIS AND IT'S ONLY OCTOBER. HE IS SMART, WELL beyond his years, and already has enough advanced course credits that will allow him to potentially graduate from college in three years instead of four. Additionally, many universities were already lining up to give him either full or partial scholarships, which meant he won't have to bother with the dreaded college applications, including the essay sections. The dilemma Pete currently faced was that he really didn't know what he wanted to do with his life, and he thought that he should, at least, have some idea before committing to a specific college.

Pete was a bit of a loner although not in an unfriendly way. He had a group of friends; however, at school he preferred spending his time learning about topics that interested him instead of participating in the daily gossip that consumed so many of his classmates. His parents constantly pushed him to go out with his friends so he could develop a better social life. Last summer, to appease his parents, he took a job in the electronics department at Southfield's. Working at the store forced him to interact with people all day long, but he also got to play around with the newest technology since Southfield's always received Collins Industries' latest and greatest gadgets. A win-win as far as he and his parents were concerned.

Pete enjoyed his time over the summer and did such a good job that his boss, Steve, asked him if he'd like to keep some hours during the school year. And, since school had become a giant yawn for Pete, he willingly accepted.

Pete got off his bike outside the service entrance of Southfield's and went inside. He punched in the code on the employee break room door and walked his bike toward the back, next to the lockers. He unlocked his u–shaped, steel lock and fastened his bike to a water pipe that ran along the cinderblock wall. This was necessary as employees had complained about personal items getting taken from the break room and Pete wasn't about to have his only current method of transportation—that is, until he saved enough for a car—disappear on him.

Pete changed into the required black, collared golf shirt with the Southfield's logo on it, tucked it into his black jeans, and headed up the back staircase to the electronics department on the second floor. His shift on Saturdays, the store's busiest day, started at 9 a.m., a full hour before the store opened.

This job had mostly been good for Pete, although, it had become a drag as of late, primarily because of Steve who seemed to be distracted on a daily basis. Pete figured he would just work there through the holiday season, make bank, and then move on to something else.

At 9:45 a.m., Steve walked into the electronics department, visibly sweating, carrying two folding chairs.

"Morning," he muttered.

"Hey, Steve. How goes it?" said Pete. Then, noticing all the perspiration, "You okay?"

"Fine. We ready to go here?" Steve asked anxiously as he looked around, seemingly ready to criticize something, anything.

"Yep. I just booted up the flat screens and laptops. The cash register should come online in a minute."

Steve put down the folding chairs and approached Pete. "Listen, we're getting a shipment of brand-new, virtual reality headsets later this morning, and I really want to use this new display case for them, okay?"

"Yeah, sure."

"Also, I'd like you to set them up so we can demo them with customers by this afternoon."

"What's the rush?"

"Because that's what Ted wants."

"You saw him?"

"This morning. There was a meeting about the new headsets."

"On a Saturday? Must be important." For Pete, this was more exciting than school any day.

"I can't say anything else."

"Can't say?" said Pete, holding out his hands. "You need my help to sell them. I need to know something about them, right?"

Steve paused for a moment, realizing that Pete was right. "That's true. I can tell you about Phase I. Phase II was the real secret over there."

"Okay, what's Phase I?"

"Phase I, or Collins VR, the real name, means that these specific virtual reality headsets can transport you almost anywhere. Or at least anywhere that's in the main database."

Pete waited for Steve to say more. "That's it? Our competitors and Collins' older products can already do that."

"I know, but they have some minor enhancements—picture quality and whatnot—and they are *the* priority over the next few weeks. I don't care if we sell a single television or camera. We need to sell one hundred of these headsets."

"That's crazy."

"I know it is, but that's what Ted wants. If possible, I'm going to need to add additional hours onto your schedule. Are you up for it? If we hit the target, I'll add a bonus on for you."

"That's fine," said Pete, now looking around. "I have some extra time, but I have to ask one thing in return."

Steve started to object, but he really needed Pete's help. "What's that?"

"Tell me about Phase II," Pete said with a grin.

Steve shook his head. "I can't, Pete."

"Oh, come on, Steve," said Pete, smiling mischievously. "I'm willing to help but you gotta tell me what the company is planning. Honestly, who am I going to tell? I spend all my free time here!"

"You don't understand, Pete. I don't know what it is. Ted wouldn't tell me. Roy and Jane, uh, the two other people at the meeting, didn't look too pleased. I can tell you that. All I know is that there is some way that these headsets can be modified and Collins is still working on it. He muttered something about a red chip." Steve shook his head. "Anyway, doesn't matter."

Again, Pete waited for more. "That's the big secret? Geez. Sorry I asked."

Steve extended his arms, shrugged, and said, "That's it, bud. What can I tell ya? Let's get ready. It'll probably be a busy day today. Saturdays usually are."

8.

THE SHIPMENT OF COLLINS VR HEADSETS WAS BROUGHT UP TO THE electronics department by Dan, one of Collins Industries' most trusted delivery guys. He pushed a flatbed cart with about six large, brown boxes precariously balanced on it.

Dan stopped the cart, pulled out a small towel, and began wiping his forehead which was covered in sweat. Never a break when delivering for Collins.

He looked up at Pete. "Man, security was giving me all kinds of issues downstairs about bringing these in now instead of after hours."

Pete, who was signing for the delivery, said, "That's Ted for ya. He's in close with the owner of this store so he pretty much gets his way."

"Don't I know it. You guys want these somewhere in particular?"

"Yeah, hang on one sec and I'll get Steve and Jaime. If you don't mind, the four of us can knock this out pretty quickly."

"Take your time, man. I can use a breather." Dan retrieved a bottle of water from his cargo shorts and took a drink.

Pete returned with Jaime, one of his co-workers, and Steve. The three of them, with Dan, put the new shipment of Collins VR headsets on an empty shelf. Pete then took two units out of their boxes and displayed them in the special case in the middle of the electronics section. These two would be used for demonstrations with customers.

As Dan was about to leave, he realized that there was a bubble envelope also included with the shipment. He looked around for Steve, didn't see him, and then checked his watch. He didn't have time to wait around.

"Pete, right?"

"Yeah. What's up?"

Dan handed Pete a large envelope and said, "One more thing. Here you go."

"Great, thanks."

"All right, buddy. You be good. Don't work too hard."

"I never do," said Pete, slapping Dan on the shoulder.

"My man," said Dan, with a smile, as he walked away.

Pete looked at the outside of the envelope and then opened it up. He assumed it went with the shipment that was just unpacked. He peered inside and pulled out a clear DVD case with a disc inside. The disc simply had "In-Store" written in red marker across it. He looked back in the envelope and pulled out two small, square black boxes and what looked like a user manual. He threw the envelope away and put the items on the counter by the cash register.

"Hey, Jaime?" said Pete. "Can you move the small flat screen and the DVD player near the display case? There is a DVD that I'm pretty sure goes with the new headsets."

"Yeah, no problem. Where's the disc?" asked Jaime.

"Here you go." Pete handed her the DVD.

"I'll double check it first before I move the TV. Cool?"

"Sure, of course. I'll be right there to help."

Pete looked back at the two black boxes, opening one out of curiosity. A Red Chip was sitting in the middle indentation. Pete started to realize that this chip could be what Steve briefly mentioned earlier. The Red Chip had two arrows pointed in a counter-clockwise direction etched on it. As Steve came around the corner, Pete quickly closed the box and put it in his pants pocket.

"What's this?" huffed Steve.

"Oh, these were in an envelope along with a DVD," said Pete, holding up the remaining items.

Steve flipped over the user manual; the cover was blank except for a large Roman numeral two printed on it. He immediately knew what he was holding.

"Uh, thanks, Pete. I'll take care of this. Why don't you give Jaime a hand?"

"Sure thing, boss."

As Pete walked away, he glanced back and watched Steve place the small box and user manual inside the cabinet, under a pile of papers. Seeing Steve's futile attempt at hiding the items, Pete now needed to see what this was all about, but would have to wait until Steve stepped away for a while, which, given his recent behavior, would happen at some point today.

9.

THE STORE'S TRAFFIC PICKED UP AS IT GOT CLOSER TO 1 P.M. SHOPPERS walked around the electronics department, mostly looking at the smart TVs and tablets.

Around 1:30 p.m., Pete got his chance to look through the user manual as Steve walked over to him in his familiar, mildly dramatic panic.

"Pete, I have to go out for a little while and there's a chance I'm gone for the rest of the day," said Steve as he put on his jacket.

"Okay, no problem."

"Don't worry. Everything will be fine," said Steve, breathing a little heavier now.

"Are you all right?"

"I'm fine. Just some family stuff. You'll be okay here?" Steve looked around the department with some concern on his face.

"Yeah, sure. Don't sweat it."

"Thanks, Pete. Remember to demo the headsets. Push a little harder if you need to, but it's important."

"Will do."

"And if you need anything—"

"Steve!" Pete placed both hands on Steve's shoulders. "Just go. Everything will be fine. I promise."

"You're right. I'll see you later."

When Steve left, Pete's shoulders dropped about an inch. Pete waited another ten minutes, retrieved the Phase II manual from the cabinet, and brought it with him to lunch. During his thirty-minute lunch break, he usually alternated among the fast food options in the mall's food court.

Twenty-nine minutes later, Pete sprinted back to the electronics department. He could not believe what he just read. He flung open the display case, removed one of the headsets, located the hidden compartment on the left side of the headset (which wasn't hidden to him anymore), and pried open the flap with a mini screwdriver that was in a drawer. He then opened the cabinet to get the Red Chip that was still under a pile of papers. He kept the second chip in his pocket but he threw the original manual back into the cabinet as he made a photocopy before returning from his break.

He inserted the chip into the headset and snapped it close. He turned on the laptop that was primarily used for checking inventory and scheduling the deliveries. Next, he downloaded the program from a special website, plugged in the wires, and started entering the information needed for the system to properly log him in, including his cell phone number. He typed in a few more commands, made a few selections on the screen, and placed the headset over his eyes. A countdown clock began is descent from "10" and a small smile formed on Pete's mouth.

Just as the counter got to "1," he was startled and brought back to reality.

"Pete?" said Jaime, tapping him on the shoulder.

"Yeah," answered Pete, pulling off the headset.

"There are a bunch of customers. Can you help me out?"

Pete looked over Jaime's head and did, in fact, now notice the many customers who must have appeared in the last ten minutes.

"Sorry. I'll be right there," said Pete anxiously as Jaime walked away.

Pete's full investigation into Phase II would need to wait a little longer. He logged out of the system, removed and returned the Red Chip to its black case, placed it back in the cabinet, and walked over to assist the waiting customers.

II.
Parker

10.

Jason

PARKER HIGH SCHOOL'S SOPHOMORE CLASS IS AN ECLECTIC MIX OF personalities and cliques. Jason Markum has grown up with most of these students and has made friends with many different groups of kids. He isn't the popular type, however—he doesn't insert himself into situations or openly flirt with girls—instead, he is level-headed, always trying to do the right thing. For example, last year, in ninth grade, his friend, Ethan, was very sick with the flu around finals time, and their science teacher, Mr. Randolph, would not grant Ethan an extension for his final exam date despite him not having the ability to study properly. Other teachers were a little more accommodating, but not Mr. Randolph. Jason knew better than to intervene directly with Mr. Randolph, who was just a straight up miserable person, and he also knew that he could help his friend in another way. Jason took the science final two days prior to Ethan's scheduled date—the finals were given based on what period each student's class was—and decided to write down as many test questions as he could on the "cheat sheet" each student was allowed to have during the exam. The cheat sheet was a three by five-inch index card and students could put as much information as they could possibly fit onto the card. The night before his exam, Jason rewrote his entire cheat sheet, deliberately leaving space throughout the card so he could easily scribble in some exam questions while also hiding them from Mr. Randolph when he would inevitably pace the room. Jason knew this was not a totally honest way to conduct himself, but when weighing that against the way Ethan was being treated simply because he was sick, Jason felt an obligation to side with his friend.

No one knew or would ever know of this except for Ethan and Jason. If word ever did get out that Jason helped Ethan, they would then both receive zeros on their final exams; a result of Mr. Randolph's zero tolerance cheating policy.

In the end, Jason helped his friend because he wanted to, not because he wanted other people to know he did. That's the type of guy he is.

11.

Southfield's, Saturday

IF THERE WAS ONE THING THAT JASON COULDN'T STAND ANYMORE, IT WAS going to the mall with his mom. Today, his mother, Debbie, has brought him to Southfield's to shoe shop and also look at the makeup and dresses that are on sale. His phone would be a welcome distraction from this boredom, but he recently got into a lot of trouble at school and his parents had taken his phone away for a week.

Jason's side of the story, as to why he got in trouble, was that it, flat out, wasn't his fault. It was Trevor's, an obnoxious kid in Jason's class. Trevor was responsible for both incidents that Jason was now being blamed for.

So, instead of hanging out with his friends, or at least scrolling through Instagram, Jason was stuck in a hot, crowded department store with techno music blasting out of the women's shoe department, with nothing to distract him except for signs about the *HUGE BLOWOUT SALE!* the store was having today.

"Jason?" his mother hollered and waved at him from across the department. "Jason! Over here! Come sit next to me while I try on these boots."

Jason slowly walked over to where his mom was sitting and plopped down in the chair next to her. He was now surrounded by what seemed like mountains of shoe boxes and women hobbling around in one shoe looking at their feet in the full-length mirrors.

"I just don't know, Jason. I feel like the size six is better in these high heels, but I would need a size seven for these boots. I wish all these shoes fit the same," said Debbie, turning her ankle while looking in the mirror.

Jason stared blankly at his mother.

She continued in a tone that suggested she was talking more to herself than to her son, "I don't really *need* two pairs of shoes, but this sale is too good. Let me see if I can find a salesperson. Wait here."

"I have to go to the bathroom," said Jason.

"Okay, I'll be right back. Watch my stuff and then you can go."

Five minutes later, Jason's mom returned with a salesperson who looked like she'd been working for the last forty-eight hours.

"Here are the two pairs of shoes—Jason! Where are the high heels and boots I was just trying on?"

Jason was slouched in the chair resting his head in his hand. "I don't know. Some guy took them away along with a bunch of other shoeboxes."

"I told you to watch my stuff!"

"I did. Your bag is right here. The shoes belong to the store."

The saleswoman tried her best to stifle a smile.

"I don't believe this. I swear, if those shoes are gone, I'm really going to be mad."

"Can I go to the bathroom now, please?"

"Just go. And take your time."

*

Jason was relieved to get out of the women's shoe jungle nightmare. He was absolutely going to take his mother's advice and take his sweet time. In fact, he might as well look around to see what other stuff this store had since he never came to Southfield's with his friends.

After going to the bathroom (he really did have to go), Jason looked in the young men's section but lost interest almost immediately. He really didn't want to look at clothes. He had a basic wardrobe that he was happy with and the idea of waiting in line to try on shirts and pants was so absurd to him, it was almost funny. Almost.

As he wandered around, he saw a sign for the electronics department on the second floor and took the escalator up. Once he got off, a smile crossed his face. Everywhere he looked, he saw smart TVs, digital cameras, laptops, phones, video games, and even fancy refrigerators with small touch screens on them.

Jason began looking up and down the aisles at all the different televisions: big, small, curved, flat, cheap, expensive. As he was making his way around, he noticed a special display case in the middle of the floor with red velvet ropes around it, just like they had around important artifacts at a museum. Inside the glass case were headsets that looked like a gigantic pair of sunglasses over a Styrofoam model of a bald, faceless, human head.

"Can I help you?" said a voice behind Jason, causing him to jump.

"Uh, no, thanks. I'm just looking at these things," said Jason.

"Things? These *things* are going to change how we see the world," said Pete in full sales mode.

"Oh, really?" replied Jason, not really believing that at all.

"Have you ever heard of virtual reality?"

Jason shrugged. "Yeah, but I don't really know much about it."

"Here." Pete punched buttons on the DVD player. "Watch this video. It's only five minutes long. I'll come over when it's done." Jason was curious and welcomed yet another distraction, so he started to watch the video.

Collins VR was the name of the virtual reality headset, and what Jason gathered from the video was that he could transport himself to a bunch of different places around the world and since his vision would be completely covered by the headset, it was like being part of the environment.

"So, what do you think?" said Pete, coming back over.

"I don't know. Seems all right, I guess," said Jason.

"All right? You're a tough one, aren't you?" said Pete, now folding his arms.

Jason mumbled, "What? I don't know."

"Well, do you want to try it on?"

Jason looked around and said, "Sure. Why not?" He had nowhere else to be.

Pete took one of the headsets out of the case and handed it to Jason.

"Go ahead and put it on. You can adjust the strap in the back so it fits correctly."

Jason put the mask over his face and tightened it like Pete said.

"I can't see anything," said Jason.

"That's correct. I have to turn it on. Hang on a sec—"

Pete plugged one end of the cable into the laptop. He then typed in a few commands and plugged the other end into the headset which was now resting on Jason's face.

"Now, what do you see?"

"Nothing yet. Wait, it looks like it's—Whoa! This is awesome!" said Jason.

The default setting on the device had him standing on the observation floor of the World Trade Center in downtown New York City on a perfectly clear day.

"Pretty cool, huh? If you turn to the left, you'll turn to the left in the simulator. The device gives three-hundred-sixty-degree views of whatever virtual world a person is in. It's a totally immersive experience," said Pete, really starting to lay it on thick.

"Just wait until we set you up with a location of your choosing. In fact, it might be better if you sit down. Many people tend to get dizzy and actually fall over when they use the device for the first time."

Pete opened a folding chair that was kept near the display for this purpose. Steve wanted to be sure he mitigated any chance of a lawsuit against Southfield's in case someone took a spill.

"Have a seat. It's right behind you."

Jason carefully reached behind him without saying a word and lowered himself into the chair. Unknowingly, his mouth was open as he took in the views of lower Manhattan.

"Pretty cool, huh? So, where do you go to school?" asked Pete.

"It's amazing. My palms are sweaty since I'm kind of afraid of heights even though I know it's not real. So freaking weird. I'm a sophomore at Parker. I'm Jason," he said as he extended his hand out in front of him.

Pete took Jason's hand and shook it. "Pete. I'm a senior at Parker. How is it I've never seen you?"

"Don't know," said Jason, not really paying attention to what Pete was saying. Pete shrugged and said, "Anyway, we only have a couple of minutes. Where else would you like to go?"

"Where else is there?"

"There are tons of options: The Amazon rainforest; Death Valley, California; Mt. Everest; the Great Pyramids. Any famous place you can think of, this device probably has it."

As Jason sat quietly, Pete leaned a little closer to Jason and whispered, "I'm not supposed to tell anyone this but if you really wanted to, there's actually a way to go back in time and watch yourself. They call it Look-Back."

Jason's ears perked up and he gently removed the mask from his face. He rubbed his eyes as they adjusted to the light.

Jason smiled skeptically, "Come on."

"I'm serious man. I just read about it earlier."

"How does it work?"

"It's new technology that's apparently still being fully developed. I haven't even tried it myself yet. It's supposed to work by pulling the data from your cellphone and then transforming it. I can set it up for us to test but it's—"

"There you are," said an unhappy Debbie walking toward her son. "Jason, I expected you to be looking at the coats, not playing video games. The coats are fifty percent off today. It's a madhouse down there. Let's go and look before there's nothing left."

Jason's face flushed from embarrassment. He turned to Pete, handing him the headset back. "Thanks, Pete. That was awesome."

"Anytime, man. This display will be here for a while. Here—" Pete reached into his pocket and handed Jason his card. "Take my card. My cell phone number is on it if you want to come back. Just text me."

"Jason? Now!"

Jason followed his mom and headed toward the escalators. He left wondering what Pete was talking about regarding this Look-Back, or whatever. He knew it had to be a gimmick to try and get him to buy the headset, but he also knew that he had to hear more.

12.

Jason's Home, Four Hours Later

APART FROM A FEW POCKETS OF HUGE HOUSES, MOST OF THE HOMES IN Oak Brook are a pretty consistent representation of suburbia USA outside of major cities. Fairly quiet neighborhoods with mailboxes at the end of driveways and two cars in each garage. The Markum's home is a three-bedroom, two-level home where Jason lives with his brother, Gregg, a senior at Parker High School, and his parents, Debbie and John.

Debbie came down the stairs and into the kitchen where Jason sat at the counter flipping through a *Wired* magazine that he convinced his mom to buy him a few hours ago in the mall.

"Okay, honey, your dad and I are going out with some friends for dinner. You and Gregg are to try not and kill each other, understood?" said Debbie.

"Yes, mom," said Jason, accustomed to his mom's theatrical requests.

"Good. Even though you're still technically grounded, you may watch TV if you'd like. Your phone, however, is still off limits. I couldn't convince your dad to budge on that one. We'll be home by 9:30."

Jason's mom gave him a quick hug and walked out of his room. The time was currently 5:50 p.m.

After his parent's left, Jason walked up the stairs and down the short hallway to his brother's room to see what he was up to. Gregg, a star athlete at Parker, had dozens of photos and varsity letters hanging all around his room. Jason recognized the sacrifices that his brother made and continued to make to play sports year-round while trying to maintain some kind of a social life. Tonight was one of those rare nights where he wasn't completely spent from a full day of practice. The school's soccer team had a week in between games and the coaches gave the players a few days off.

Gregg was looking out his window through an opening in the blinds.

"Going somewhere?" said Jason.

"Whoa!" said Gregg, startled. "Try knocking first, dork."

Jason knocked on the doorframe. "Going somewhere?"

"Yeah, out." Gregg walked over to the full-length mirror that hung inside his closet door.

"Where?"

"Don't worry about it."

"What am I supposed to do?"

"You heard mom. Watch TV," said Gregg, now fixing his hair and trying to look at his profile.

"Let me come with you," pleaded Jason.

Gregg laughed. "No chance. I'm hanging out with some friends. Just stay here and don't set the house on fire. Now get out. Ray's brother is picking me up in ten minutes."

Jason walked out of his brother's room. Being grounded was the worst and now he didn't even have his older brother around to hang out with. Gregg may not be the friendliest guy on the planet but he's not the meanest either. Underneath all the occasional bravado, Gregg really did care about Jason; he just kept quiet about it most of the time.

After Gregg left for the night, Jason grabbed a bottled water and the turkey sandwich his mom left for him, turned on the television in the living room, and plunked down on the couch. As he clicked through the channels, his thoughts started to, once again, drift back to the headsets at Southfield's from a few hours earlier.

Jason now began playing a mental tug of war as a new, slightly risky idea came to him. *Why couldn't I go out?* Jason thought. *I can get to Southfield's on my bike in about twenty-*

five minutes. *But I would be in so much trouble if they found out. But, then again, I need to talk to Pete about the Look-Back feature. It's crazy, but what if that device can actually get me off the hook at school since no one seems to want to hear my side of the story?* Jason's options were severely limited. He was also bored and losing his mind without his phone and this technology, that he really knew nothing about, seemed like a perfectly logical way to try and fix what happened.

Jason turned off the television, wolfed down the rest of his sandwich, chugged the water, and then ran up to his room to plan out the expedition. He debated calling a friend or two to see if they wanted to join, but there was something about this whole thing that he wanted to keep to himself. He quickly changed and went back down to the kitchen to draw up his detailed plan for the night. No detail was too small; he *had* to make sure that he was back well before 9:30 p.m. If he wasn't ... actually, he didn't even want to entertain those consequences right now.

The time was now 6:33 p.m. and Gregg was long gone. Jason thought again, *If I leave at 6:45, I can easily get to the mall by 7:15. I would then need to lock up my bike and make my way back to the second floor of Southfield's. Let's call that 7:25. As long as no one else is testing out the headsets, I can spend ten minutes begging Pete to tell me more about the Look-Back and then hopefully try it out for real. This assumes that Pete is still working. Anyway, if I can do all of this by 8:15 and leave immediately, I can make it home and shower well before they come home. Easy.*

Of course, this plan also assumed that nothing would go wrong along the way.

Jason grabbed another water bottle from the fridge and went into the garage to get his bike. He opened the garage door, fastened his helmet, and as he was about to pedal away, heard the house phone ring.

He quickly jumped off his bike and ran inside to answer it. Jason knew it was his mom calling. If no one answered the phone, she would immediately begin to worry and would, no doubt, call again. Thank God he hadn't left yet. His plan would have been ruined before it even had a chance.

"Hello?" said Jason.

"Hi, honey. It's Mom. How are you?"

Jason rolled his eyes. He obviously knew it was her, but she always reiterates that "It's Mom."

"I'm good."

"What are you up to?"

"Uh, just ate and was about to watch a movie," Jason lied as he looked around the room.

"That's nice. Which one?"

"Not sure yet." Jason motioned with his arms for his mom to get to the point already.

"Okay. Anyway, there's a frozen chicken in the downstairs freezer for dinner tomorrow. It's buried under a bunch of pizzas and vegetables. Do me a favor and just take it out and leave it on the kitchen counter. It needs to start defrosting."

"I'll do it now." Jason was staring at the clock. Every second counted in his plan and he was in no mood for this chit-chat.

Additionally, he knew that if he didn't get out the door soon, he was likely to talk himself out of the whole thing.

"Thanks, honey. Our table's ready. Love you. Bye." The phone had already clicked before Jason could say goodbye in return.

Jason decided to deal with the chicken later. He was already behind schedule and hadn't even left the house yet. He went back into the garage, hopped on his bike, closed the garage, and flew down the driveway on his way to the mall.

The time was now 6:52 p.m. The roads were quiet and dark as he pedaled along the side streets on his way up to the main road. This moment of peace gave him time to think more about how the punishment served to him at school could not stand. Additionally, redemption seemed unattainable given the way Trevor operated. When putting Trevor's word against his own, Trevor would be the one who was heard and not Jason. A lot of that had to do with his father, who seemed to be friends with *everyone* in Oak Brook.

Jason biked onto the main road where, fortunately, there was a sidewalk so he didn't have to be in the street with the cars and trucks whizzing by. He still needed to be alert, though, because the fallen leaves tend to cover large sticks and cracks in the sidewalk and he really didn't want to take a header over his bike's handlebars tonight. As he approached the center of town, he rode past a convenience store where there were a bunch of bikes parked out front. Jason came to a stop in the parking lot in front of the store and checked his watch. 7:12 p.m. *Not too bad*, he thought.

He recognized a couple of friends by their bikes and decided to see what they were up to since he had a minute or two to spare. As he approached, some of the guys looked up and were surprised to see him as they all knew he was grounded.

They exchanged some small talk when Rob, a tall, athletic kid, and a friend of Jason's, came out of the store and interrupted, "Hey, dude, what're you doing here?"

"I had to run into town to get my mom something," Jason lied again.

"That's cool."

The group then stuffed all of their newly bought candy into their pockets and picked up their bikes to head out. Rob then said, "Lori, you coming? We're heading to Little Sicily for pizza. Hey man, you can come too."

"Sorry, I can't," Jason quickly answered.

"Not tonight, Rob. I'm gonna head home," said Lori.

"You sure?" said Rob.

"Yeah, I'll see you guys on Monday."

"See ya Monday," Rob shrugged and said as he hopped on his bike and rode off with the others.

Lori was putting on her helmet when Jason walked over to her. Lori and Jason were classmates and have been friends for many years. Lori also knew all about Jason getting in trouble earlier in the week.

Jason straddled his bike and said, "Hey, why didn't you go with those guys?"

Lori shrugged. "I don't know. Just didn't feel like it tonight. What are you getting for your mom?"

Jason looked down and said, "Nothing, actually. My parents don't know I'm out. I was going to Southfield's to check something. I was there earlier today with my mom. She made me go with her because of some sale. I didn't even get anything, except a headache. That place sucks."

"I hate that store," said Lori.

"Oh," Jason said, with a hint of disappointment in his voice.

"What?" said Lori, smiling and playfully kicking him in the shin.

"I have to go now to get back home before my parents do. Do you want to come?"

"You shopping or something?"

"No, I ... I saw something in the electronics section earlier that I need to go back and see. It's going to sound bizarre. You wanna hear it? I can give you the super short version."

"Sure."

Jason finished telling Lori the quick, two-minute version of his trip to Southfield's earlier that day when she said bluntly, "The Look-Back sounds totally ridiculous, Jason. I mean, come on, time travel? Do you hear yourself?"

Jason shook his head. "I know it sounds insane, but why not check it out?"

Lori was now looking down at the ground. "I don't know. Hanging out sounds cool and all, but I should probably get home."

"We won't be there long. We'll try it out and then leave. Hopefully Pete is there and isn't too busy."

"Who's Pete?"

Jason checked his watch and then looked back at Lori smiling, and said, "You'll see."

After another moment, Lori strapped on her helmet and started to ride off. Jason was about to say something when she looked back and said, "Hey, Markum? We going or what?"

13.

JASON AND LORI WERE TEN MINUTES INTO THE REMAINDER OF THE TRIP when the road started becoming more and more crowded with cars. Fortunately, a pedestrian tunnel allowed people to either walk or ride their bikes underneath the main road. Jason and Lori rode single file through the tunnel and came out in the Southfield's parking lot. They cycled over to a bike rack that was hidden out of view from the main entrance, locked their bikes, and went into the store.

Jason and Lori walked quickly along the first floor toward the escalators. As they got on, there were several people in front of the them. Once off the escalator on the second floor, they went directly to the display case by the electronics.

The electronics department was much quieter than it was earlier. However, the other parts of the store were still plenty busy with the continuing sales.

A voice called out from behind them.

"So, you're back for some more fun?"

Jason, relieved to see he was still working, said, "Hey, Pete!"

Pete smiled, "Hey, Jason. I didn't expect to see you tonight. Or I thought you would shoot me a text."

"I don't have my phone at the moment and I *need* to see the thing you started to tell me about when my mom came over and interrupted. By the way, this is my friend, Lori. I came to show her the headsets, too."

Pete shook Lori's hand. "Good to meet you. Jason's told me nothing about you. Give me one minute. I just need to restock something. Be right back."

Pete disappeared down an aisle and Jason and Lori waited for him to return.

"Interesting guy," quipped Lori, and then jokingly said, "I thought for sure you would have told him all about me and how amazing I am. I'm pretty upset now."

"Very funny. He's cool. Just a bit quirky. He's actually a senior at our school. I have never seen him, though," said Jason.

"Me neither."

Jason and Lori were looking at the headsets through the glass case when Jason started telling Lori about the virtual reality headset and being on the top of the World Trade Center.

"It's awesome. The picture is crystal clear, and you can see out three-hundred and sixty degrees just by turning like you would if you were actually standing up there," said Jason.

"That's pretty sweet. I've never been to the World Trade Center. Would love to go, though," said Lori.

Pete then returned, opened the glass case, and removed the two headsets.

"Okie Dokie. Let's get you two wired up," said Pete.

Jason, looking at the headsets, asked, "What do you mean?"

"The stuff I told you about earlier only scratches the surface of what these babies can do. You can actually sync up to five of these headsets so everyone is in the same world."

"Seriously?"

"Yeah, man."

Pete began assembling both headsets, including plugging in the power cords and connecting the cables. When he finished, both headsets had two long, black wires coming out of each of them.

"Okay, a few things before we start," said Pete, holding both headsets. "Number one, if you feel dizzy or lightheaded, there are two folding chairs right behind you. I suggest you sit down immediately so you don't fall over and get hurt. I'll also get in a ton of trouble if that happens. Got it?"

Jason and Lori both responded, "Got it."

Pete continued, "Number two, for whatever reason, when people put these things on, they feel the need to shout at each other. You don't need to do that. You're still standing right next to each other so keep your voices at this level. Cool?"

"Cool," they responded.

"And finally, three, the same rules and laws apply in the virtual world as they do here. If you try anything illegal or do anything dangerous, the system will automatically shut off and will not let you back in for twenty-four hours. In short, don't be an idiot."

"A full day? That's pretty rough," said Lori.

"I agree. There is an override, but it looks like a pain to set up. Are we good on all three rules?"

Pete looked at Jason. "We're good."

Pete looked at Lori. "Yep, all good. Let's do it."

"Okay, great. Let's give this a whirl."

Pete handed each of them the headsets and they put them on. Pete walked behind them and tightened each headset so it was snug and then walked back over to the laptop. He started typing.

"I just see black," said Lori.

"That's correct," said Pete. "Gimme two seconds. I need to load this up. Jason, you want New York City again or somewhere else?"

Jason replied, "Let's do New York again. I want Lori to see the view and I kinda want to see it again, too."

"Okay, you got it. You should see it ... now," said Pete as he punched the Enter key on the keyboard.

A few seconds later, Lori's mouth fell open and she immediately began to wobble.

"Whoa! I've never been up this high before. COOL ... THERE'S THE STATUE OF LIBERTY!"

"Shh," said Pete with a smirk. "Remember, we're still in the store."

Lori, in a whisper, replied, "Oh, sorry. It's just unbelievable!"

Jason said, "I told you. Let's walk over here. Hey, Pete, how do we walk?"

"Just point to where you want to go and start marching in place."

"Lori, you see the window facing the Empire State Building?" said Jason.

"Yeah."

"Let's both point at it and head over there."

Lori turned to her right. "I see it. So, I just raise my hand up now?"

"I think so."

"Okay, I'm pointing at the window."

"Me too. Let's starts marching in place. Slowly."

Jason and Lori marched in place with their right arms extended in front of them. There were several shoppers walking by who could not help but look at the two peculiar kids in the middle of the electronics department, marching in place like soldiers, with large headsets covering half their faces.

Pete, looking up from his laptop, smiled and said, "You don't have to keep holding your arms up. In fact, you don't even have to keep marching. The system understands where you want to go just by pointing and taking a couple of steps. It won't let you walk into the window or fall down a staircase or anything like that."

"Got it," said Jason.

A few more minutes passed by and Jason and Lori pointed out different landmarks from their view from the World Trade Center. They could see the Brooklyn Bridge to the right, the George Washington Bridge slightly to the left and farther away, and Central Park right in the middle of Manhattan.

Jason then asked, "HEY, PETE, WHEN CAN WE SEE THE TIME TRAVEL STUFF?"

Several shoppers looked over at the loud comment and Pete, who was now visibly irritated, looked up from his screen again and then at some of the shoppers. He approached Jason.

"Dude. That hasn't launched yet. Keep your voice down. In fact, let's take these masks off. I think that's enough for tonight."

Pete returned to the laptop and punched in a few keys and the screens on the devices faded to black. Jason and Lori removed the masks and handed them back to Pete. It took a second for their eyes to adjust to the bright store lighting and they both sat down in the folding chairs.

"I'm a little dizzy. Sorry again for yelling, Pete," said Jason.

"It's cool man. *Everyone* does it the first time."

"What can you tell us about the Look-Back?"

Pete sighed. "I shouldn't have even said anything earlier. It's a dumb habit I have. Whenever I find out a secret, I can't keep it. I always seem to find a reason to trust the person I'm speaking with about it, even if I just met them, like with you earlier today."

"We're not going to tell anyone. C'mon man. I'm risking life in prison for this." Jason's mom's theatrics clearly were having an effect.

"That's a bit dramatic," said Lori, laughing slightly.

"Guys, the info was literally handed to me by a delivery guy this morning and, like I said, it's new technology that's not out yet and I wasn't even supposed to find out. For now, it can supposedly only transport people back one month, max."

"You do realize how crazy that sounds, right?" said Jason.

"Yeah, no way it can do that," said Lori dismissively.

"I'm serious, guys. I read the manual earlier. It's right here under the counter," said Pete pointing to the cabinet under the laptop where Steve placed it earlier that day.

"There's a manual? Let's see it," said Jason.

"Forget it," said Pete, smiling.

"So, just tell us the basics. How does it work?" Lori nudged.

Pete sighed again. The effects of a long day and their persistence wore on him, and he realized that he needed to give them something. He picked up one of the masks and pointed to an area on the left side.

"You see this little slit here that's kinda hidden and the small hinge here?"

Jason and Lori looked closely and nodded.

"Well, it opens but you need a small screwdriver or something similar to pry it up. Here, let me show you."

Pete reached back, grabbed the mini screwdriver he used earlier, and opened the flap.

"Now, you see this circular indentation here?"

Lori replied, "Yeah."

"Well, there's a red, circular disc, a computer chip, essentially, that snaps into that hole. This Red Chip supposedly changes the whole system."

"How?"

"The manual says that the sensors in the chip connect with sensors in the helmet. You then input your cell phone number into the special program that you first need to download onto a laptop. The system then uses *that* personal information to transport you back in time. It's not perfect and the screen images are not as clear as what you just saw looking out of the windows of the World Trade Center, but it's still supposed to be legit. One of the chips is actually in that cabinet behind you."

"I dunno, Pete. That sounds like a straight up gimmick," said Lori.

"Can we try it to see if it really works?" said Jason.

"That's not a good idea. I'll get into a ton of trouble if my boss notices and, like I said, I haven't even tried it myself so, you're right Lori, it could be a dud. Besides, why wouldn't you just want to explore all those other places around the world? To me, that's so much better than going back to where you once were," said Pete, trying to downplay the time travel in hopes that Lori and Jason would drop the subject.

Jason felt a little bummed out since he went to all this trouble and said, "It's just that ... there was this thing that happened at school last Monday that I got in trouble for. It wasn't my fault and I'm still technically grounded. If my parents knew I snuck out of the house to come here, they're going to be beyond pissed."

"Geez, man. What did you do?" said Pete.

"Nothing! That's the thing. It was this other guy in our class who gets away with everything. I saw him do *both* things and then he blamed me, and I, of course, got in trouble. It's ridiculous," said Jason.

"Why didn't you say something then?"

"I tried to. The principal, Mr. Hagen, wouldn't even listen. Like I said, no one ever seems to blame Trevor for whatever reason. It just doesn't make any sense."

"Mr. Hagen is still pretty new at the school, but it's weird that he didn't hear you out, though. What exactly happened?"

Jason sighed. "I don't know if I have time to tell it."

Lori looked at Jason's watch. "It's 8:23. If you're going to make it home, we'll need to go pretty soon."

"I know."

"Just give me the short version," said Pete, smiling. "I told you about this chip, you owe me a good story."

"Just tell him, Jason."

Jason paused, realizing he was stuck, and then began to tell the story. "All right. It all started last Monday during biology..."

14.
The Incident, Monday, Five Days Ago

MONDAY MORNINGS WERE THE EXTENDED BIOLOGY CLASS THAT everyone dreaded. The class went from 8:30 a.m. to 11:00 a.m. with only one ten-minute break in the middle.

Jason was nervous about this particular class because they were all getting their quizzes back from the prior week. The class was learning about the anatomies of different mammals and Jason was having a hard time remembering the material. The teacher said that she would hand back the quizzes after the break and then they would all review them together. She also mentioned that she was disappointed with the class's overall results, which immediately made Jason's stomach hurt.

The clock seemed to tick slowly as the only break approached. Shortly before the break, Mrs. Goldfeather, the biology teacher, called on Jason to read a paragraph in the textbook aloud to the class, but his mind had wandered off to some foreign place.

"Excuse me, Jason? Would you mind paying attention?" said Mrs. Goldfeather.

"Huh? Oh, sorry," answered Jason, mortified.

The class giggled, including Trevor, who then said something under his breath causing a few of the kids around him to laugh again.

"Third paragraph down. Please read clearly." Mrs. Goldfeather then looked at Trevor, and said, "Trevor, knock it off."

Jason put his face in the book and read the words aloud. His cheeks flushed with embarrassment. Students would get caught daydreaming from time to time but it had never happened to him before.

Jason finished the paragraph and Mrs. Goldfeather gave the class their long-awaited break. She then told the class that she needed to run down to the office for a moment and would be right back. Some kids took parts of their lunch from their bags and started wolfing down sandwiches, crackers, cookies, and whatever else they brought with them. There was something about Monday mornings and this class that caused everyone to be hungrier earlier than usual. They had to eat quickly because food was forbidden in the biology classroom, more than likely because of all the formaldehyde and other nasty chemicals seemingly stuck to everything. Other kids lined up to go to the bathroom down the hall. Boys and girls could each only go one at a time, which annoyed the students to no end. Mrs. Goldfeather used to teach in the elementary school and apparently carried some of those rules with her to the high school.

Jason was waiting in line for the bathroom when he noticed Trevor casually walk up to Mrs. Goldfeather's desk. Trevor glanced around to see if anyone was watching him and then moved a notebook, bent down, and started rifling through pages on her desk. Another student, Benny, walked up to Trevor, said something, and proceeded to walk to the classroom door.

"Hey, back of the line, Benny. I'm about to explode," said one of the students near the front.

"Relax. I'm not in line. I'm just waiting for Mrs. Goldfeather," said Benny, as he rotated glances between Trevor and the hallway.

Jason was furious. Maybe it was the embarrassment from a few minutes ago, but something compelled him to take matters into his own hands and confront Trevor. Besides, he didn't need the whole class knowing his probable lousy grade.

While the other kids scarfed down snacks and talked in small groups, Jason made his way to the front of the classroom. Trevor was so engrossed in searching through the stack of papers that he didn't even see Jason standing right next to him.

"What are you doing?" said Jason, startling Trevor.

"Uh, nothing. Get out of here, man," replied Trevor nervously, motioning him away with his head.

"You shouldn't be doing that."

"Mind your business, geek." Trevor continued to flip through the quizzes.

"Mind *my* business? You're looking at everyone's grades!"

Some students started to watch what was unfolding between these two.

"Don't worry, you didn't fail," said Trevor with a grin on his face. "Now, get away from me."

This was how Trevor operated. He constantly kept his classmates in fear of being embarrassed by using their own personal details, like quiz scores, against them. He would somehow uncover various details while also subtly letting his classmates know he possessed the information. In this particular instance, he was well aware that all eyes were on him as he rifled through the papers, memorizing the names with the lower grades for use at a later time.

Benny, on the other hand, was just a spineless accomplice. Despite being threatened by Trevor in the past, he knew it was safer on Trevor's side when he decided to go on one of his bullying rampages.

A moment later, Benny walked toward Jason and Trevor, waving his hands in front of him with a look of panic on his face, when Mrs. Goldfeather returned.

"Excuse me, gentlemen!" yelled Mrs. Goldfeather from the doorway, her booming voice echoing off the classroom walls.

The entire class froze and all conversations immediately stopped.

"Everyone sit down!"

The entire class quickly returned to their seats, including Trevor and Jason.

"Not you two. You stand right there."

Two kids were walking into the classroom, laughing, and immediately stopped when they observed the current situation. They practically ran to their seats after seeing the faces of the rest of the class.

Mrs. Goldfeather looked at Jason and Trevor who were now standing shoulder to shoulder.

"I am not going to take my valuable class time to discuss what you two were just doing at my desk. It looks like you were going through everyone's quizzes, which is outrageous and none of your business. Both of you sit down and do not discuss anything that you might have seen. Do you understand?"

Trevor spoke up. "Mrs. Goldfeather, it was Ja—"

"Quiet. I said not a word. Now go sit down."

Jason and Trevor quietly returned to their desks. Trevor had the same grin on his face as before until he turned back around to face Mrs. Goldfeather, at which time the look disappeared. Jason stewed at his desk, his hands shaking from a combination of anger and embarrassment.

The entire sophomore class had lunch from 11:30 a.m. to noon and then, because of the shortened week, the students were allowed to go outside during their usual study hall period. On this day, Jason and a bunch of his friends decided to play basketball on the blacktop right outside of the cafeteria. The makeshift basketball court—a hoop, minus the net, on an ancient, metal backboard that was affixed to a brick wall—sat on the right side of the building. The space was typically used as an overflow parking lot when there were events held at the school. In the front of the school was a long, U-shaped driveway with an entrance at one end and an exit at the other. In between the driveway and the road was where the teachers' parking lot was located. The parking lot was visible from the back part of the "basketball court." For school liability reasons, students were not allowed to go into the teachers' parking lot unless given permission by a safety officer—off-duty police officers hired by the school as an extra security measure.

Jason normally enjoyed playing basketball with his friends, but today was different. The incident with Mrs. Goldfeather, and his subsequent embarrassment, still hung on his mind.

"Hey, Jason. Pay attention," said Jason's friend, Rob, bouncing the ball to him.

"What?" said Jason, broken out of yet another daydream. "Oh, sorry." This time, though, something caught his eye in the teachers' parking lot.

"What's with you, man? Forget about Mrs. Goldfeather. It wasn't your fault. Nothing's going to happen."

Jason ignored that last comment and pointed at something in the parking lot and said, "Check it out. What's Trevor doing over *there*?"

Rob turned around and looked. "Who knows? He's such a suck up to the teachers, he's probably cleaning out one of their cars for them."

Jason laughed but knew that wasn't it. Trevor might be a suck up to some, but he wouldn't help a blind, elderly woman cross the street, much less do a favor for a teacher. Jason also knew that his classmates would not have his back and speak out against Trevor given the lengths he will go to get revenge on anyone who tries to make him look bad.

The other kids playing basketball were getting restless and Jason just shrugged and continued on with the game. After a few minutes, though, he looked over again and noticed Trevor was now ducking behind a car.

"Here," said Jason as he threw the ball to Rob. "Just play without me. I'll be right back."

"You're not supposed to be over there," Rob yelled to Jason.

"I'm sure Trevor isn't either," Jason called back.

Jason jogged across the driveway into the parking lot, drawing the attention of one of the safety officers at the other end of the property. As he approached a red sedan, he could no longer see Trevor. He then peered around the backside of the car and noticed Trevor on the ground near one of the tires.

"What are you doing now?" said Jason, holding out his arms.

"Nothing, man," said Trevor, noticeably startled. "Mrs. Goldfeather mentioned she dropped something and I was just looking to see if it was here. Why are you on my back today?"

"This is her car?"

"Yeah, I think so."

"Why is her back tire flat?" Jason said, pointing to the back, left tire.

"Is it?"

"Look at it. The front one is as well! Did you do this?" Jason's face turned red.

Trevor looked down and said calmly, "Are you sure? They might be a little low, but I don't think they're flat."

Jason then knelt down and pushed against the sidewall of the tire. As he was doing this, Trevor took a tire pressure gauge, which had the shape of a regular pen, out of his pocket and slipped it into Jason's pants pocket without him noticing.

95

A few seconds later, Manny, one of the safety officers, appeared. At school, the officers went by their first names as opposed to the more formal "Officer Thompson," in this case. The school felt it helped the students see the officers as buddies who were there to look out for them, not to intimidate them.

"What are you two doing?" said Manny in an even tone with his hands on his hips.

Trevor spoke immediately. "I just saw Jason over here and it looks like he was flattening the tires on this car."

"What?" Jason shot back. "I just caught you!" Then, turning to face Manny, "Manny, listen to me—"

"Don't lie, Jason," answered Trevor.

"I'm not! Are you kidding me?"

"Guys, stop. One or both of you did something here," said Manny with his hands out in front of him. "First of all, you both know that you should not be over here at all. Secondly, whoever did do this is in a world of trouble. Vandalism on school property is not tolerated one bit. This is a *teacher's* car."

Trevor spoke again, "I think it's Mrs. Goldfeather's."

Jason shot back, "You see? Why would he know that?"

"Because you just told me," said Trevor grinning again as Manny knelt down to get a closer look at the tire.

"Manny. This is insane. I was playing basketball with my friends and saw him over here. It looked suspicious so I came over."

"Why didn't you come and tell me so I could check it out?" said Manny.

"What? I don't know. Because it was right across the driveway and I just walked over," said Jason, wide-eyed and breathing heavy.

"You know you're not supposed to be over here." Manny folded his arms showcasing his massive forearms.

"Well, he's not supposed to be flattening tires!"

"Calm down," said Manny.

"Manny, look," said Trevor in a measured tone. "Jason had an incident with Mrs. Goldfeather this morning, and it seems like he's trying to get back at her. I saw him using a pen or something that looked like one to let the air out. Check his pockets. Here, look at mine."

Trevor inverted his two pant pockets and pulled out the contents. "See? Nothing but a used tissue and a house key."

Manny looked at Trevor and then at Jason.

"What's in your pockets, Jason?"

Jason reached in and felt something unfamiliar. He slowly pulled out the tire gauge.

"*Trevor* was using this!" exclaimed Jason, pointing the tire gauge at Trevor. "He obviously put it in my pocket." Jason was beside himself. As before, his hands started to shake and he could feel the rush of blood to his head.

"All right, enough. Both of you come with me. We need to report this, now."

"This is such bull," muttered Jason.

"You can tell Mr. Hagen all about it. I'm sorry, Jason but I can't ignore what I just saw."

"I'm happy to tell Mr. Hagen what *I* just saw," said Trevor.

"I'm sure you are, Trevor," said Manny as they walked toward the school's main entrance.

All three sat inside the office waiting for Mr. Hagen, the school principal. His assistant, Shirley, had them wait on the couch usually reserved for visitors. Manny sat in between Jason and Trevor and no one said a word.

Roger Hagen has only been at Parker High School since the beginning of the school year. He is relatively young, but has already held various administrative roles in middle schools in Rhode Island, including a three-year stint as vice-principal. This was his first time both as a principal and working in a high school. He was of average height with short black hair and a friendly face. He was also always impeccably dressed in a suit and tie, even on hot days. His inexperience brought both positives and challenges to the position. The parents liked him because he was a breath of fresh air from the previous principal who did not deviate from the same schedule and talking points for the last fifteen years. Yet, his seeming inability to propose changes that parents have been suggesting, even demanding for years, had also been a source of frustration. Other than an initial encouraging letter to all of the parents about how he wanted to modernize the school in terms of technology and certain administrative functions, there hasn't been any movement in that direction. And while it was only a few months, many parents were eager to see Parker High join the neighboring towns in coming up to speed with their school system.

*

After a few minutes, Mr. Hagen appeared, looked over at them, and said to Shirley, "What's this all about?"

Shirley, staring at her computer, said, "Manny brought them in a few minutes ago. There's been an incident out in the teacher's parking lot."

Mr. Hagen sighed and looked at the clock. "Ten minutes before classes start again. Manny, you and Trevor come in here first. Jason, please wait a few minutes and then we'll speak."

Jason just looked away. Anger had once again taken over his emotions, but he knew enough to just keep quiet until he could state his case. Raising his voice, especially to the principal who's known him for only a few months, wasn't going to win him any favors. Trevor was obviously playing a dirty game and Jason wasn't about to sink to his level.

Exactly ten minutes later, Mr. Hagen appeared. He called Jason in and then he walked over to speak with Shirley about some other issue. Manny escorted Trevor back to his class through a second door in the principal's office.

Mr. Hagen's office was drab and depressing. He clearly had not found the time to redecorate since taking over the position. The cinder block walls were covered in faded, yellow paint and had rickety shelving that held various books, some of which were already partially dust covered, and trinkets on display to try and give the office some personality. One thing that caught Jason's eye, though, was a glass jar filled with seashells. He began wondering where those shells came from and who collected them. Also, from the pictures in the frames around the room, it seemed like he was married and had two daughters.

"Have a seat," bellowed Mr. Hagen as he stepped into his office and closed the door. The bell signaled the students back to class. He sat down and leaned back in his chair. "So, what happened?"

Jason was nervous and his mouth was now dry. "Mr. Hagen, I didn't do anything. It was all Trevor. I saw him in the parking lot, walked over, and noticed he was on the ground near one of Mrs. Goldfeather's tires. I confronted him about it and then Manny walked over. This was when Trevor must have placed that thing in my pocket."

"So, you're saying that Trevor not only let the air out of the tires, but that he also planted evidence? I think you're watching too many police shows on television, Jason."

"Planted evidence?"

"It's an expression that's sometimes used when people claim they were set up. Isn't it also true that the two of you had a bit of a situation in Mrs. Goldfeather's class a couple of hours ago?"

"Yes, but—"

"Jason, do you see where I'm going with this? It doesn't look very good. Vandalizing a teacher's car, on school property no less, is a serious matter."

"But it wasn't me! Why doesn't anyone believe me?" said Jason, raising his now quivering voice slightly and leaning back in his chair.

"You were seen next to the car and you had the tire gauge." Mr. Hagen picked up the green tire gauge and held it up. "As you know, this checks the tire pressure in cars but can also release the air."

"No, I don't know that. I've never seen that before."

"Why didn't you just tell Manny?"

"I don't know. Maybe if he was nearby, I would have. I didn't even think about it. I saw something that didn't look right and I went over to see what it was."

Mr. Hagen smirked. "Looks like we have a young vigilante in the tenth grade."

"A what?"

"A vigi— forget it. That's enough for now." Mr. Hagen scribbled a note on a pad, tore it off, and handed it to Jason. "Here, bring this to your next teacher. I have to think this over. If I were you, I'd lay low for the next couple of days. I'll have to contact your parents in the meantime."

Jason took the note from Mr. Hagen and quietly exited the office.

15.
Southfield's, Saturday night, 8:43 p.m.

ON BUSY DAYS AND NIGHTS, THE WALL OUTLETS IN SOUTHFIELD'S ARE fully utilized with phones plugged into the sockets, owners hovering nearby. On this particular night, every single one of the outlets in the women's shoe department and the nearby coat section, which started to display winter coats, was taken.

Some of these outlets were hidden from view which was really the ideal location, especially on days like today when there was more than the normal amount of people in the store because of the *HUGE BLOWOUT SALE!*

It was in one of these hidden alcoves that the fire started. There was a sense of complacency about watching over their phones (and the outlet) that came over the mother and daughter shopping that caused them to walk away, if only briefly, leaving stacks of shoe boxes and loose tissue paper too close to the overheated phones resting on the floor.

It must have been the power surge that triggered the chaos because, in a brief moment, the lights flashed in the store and all of the shoppers, almost in unison, let out a collective "Whoa!" yet no one noticed the smoke that the shoebox tissue paper was giving off. In thirty seconds, the fire department would later determine, the tissue paper ignited and subsequently lit a stack of shoeboxes on fire. From there the fire found its way along the floor, littered with tissue paper and paper shopping bags, until it reached the parkas, with faux fur along their hoods, that were hanging only a few feet away. That is when the alarms went off in the entire store.

Southfield's fire alarms made an incredibly unpleasant, piercing sound that came just as Jason finished his retelling of "The Incident" to Lori and Pete. All three stood up and looked around the store at the hordes of people now running for the exits. Little kids were crying, parents were shouting, and there was a rush of people trying get down the escalator which was now switched off. Strobe lights were flashing on almost every support column, and the fire sprinklers started to erupt all over the store.

Pete looked around and turned to Jason and Lori saying, "You two should get out of here. One quick thing to really help me out. In that cabinet is a big piece of brown plastic. Can you just throw it over the laptop and cash register?"

"Sure," said Lori, looking around and starting to freak out a little because of the chaos.

"Jason, text me when you get home," said Pete.

"I can't. I don't have my phone," said Jason, also looking around at the madness growing in the store.

"I'll text you, Pete. What's your number?" said Lori, pulling out her phone.

Pete fished another business card out of his pocket and handed it to Lori. "Here. My personal number is on the back." He then looked at the headsets that Jason and Lori were still holding. "Can you just toss those in the cabinet? I'll take care of them later. Good luck, Jason. I gotta go."

Pete disappeared into the fray to help his coworkers salvage whatever electronics they could while more fire sprinklers popped open like champagne bottles all around the second floor, including near where they were standing.

Jason and Lori looked at each other and then down at the headsets. Lori handed her headset to Jason and then turned and knelt to look under the cabinet for the plastic that Pete mentioned. She found it folded up underneath a pile of scattered papers.

"Throw those in here," Lori instructed.

Jason placed the headsets in the cabinet as water was now raining down on them. They unfolded the brown tarp and draped it over the laptop and the cash register. The tarp was so big that it fell all the way down to the floor on either side. Lori went underneath the tarp as Jason was looking around for the nearest exit.

Jason shouted at Lori, "Come on. Let's get out of here. There's an emergency exit door in the corner."

After a few seconds, Lori reappeared. "I'm ready. Let's go."

Jason and Lori sprinted toward the exit through what seemed like a rain storm. Security guards, squinting from the water pelting their faces, shouted at people to move quickly but to also remain calm. The employees working behind the jewelry cases took the display merchandise and threw it into the glass cases to prevent the pieces from getting ruined by the water.

Jason had never experienced something like this, and it only occurred to him now that the building could actually be on fire. His mind refocused as he and Lori escaped into the emergency exit stairwell and quickly walked down the stairs. Once on the ground floor, the stairwell exited into the parking lot which was now total mayhem. Cars were pointed in different directions, horns were blaring, and drivers were jockeying for position to get to the exits. People were shouting at each other while carefully managing their way in between the cars to their own vehicles.

Jason and Lori had to get their bearings to figure out where their bikes were locked up since they came out a different way than they went in.

"This way," said Lori, running from Jason.

"You sure?" said Jason, calling after her.

"Pretty sure."

Lori was right. They found their bikes, unlocked them quickly, fastened their helmets, and walked the bikes back to the tunnel as it was too dangerous to try and ride in between the cars. They eventually got to the tunnel, hopped on their bikes, and rode through.

16.

9:01 p.m., Twenty-nine minutes until Jason's parents return

As THEY EMERGED OUT OF THE TUNNEL, THE MAIN ROAD WAS LITTERED with traffic as the police started to close off the roads that passed by the mall. Jason and Lori looked back and could see firetrucks heading toward the backside of the mall.

"Let's get away from here," said Lori.

"Yeah. I have to fly in order to beat my parents home. I'll catch up with you this weekend. Those headsets were pretty cool, huh?"

"They were. Thanks for taking me along. I would love to try the time travel stuff to see if it even works."

"Agreed. We'll talk more." Then noticing the shopping bag Lori was now holding, "What's in the bag?"

"It's nothing. Good luck!" said Lori as she rode away with the shopping bag swinging on her forearm.

Jason shrugged and said almost inaudibly, "Thanks." He then pedaled away.

*

Jason's legs and lungs were burning as he made his way back along the main road. He was in decent shape for a fifteen-year-old boy, though, riding at this level of intensity with a headful of guilt was exhausting. Jason tried to keep looking at his watch to check the time, but the side of the road he was now on was also a mess with sticks and leaves and therefore, once again, demanded his full attention. He was confident that if he kept up his current pace, though, he would make it home in time. The only unknown question was whether his parents would arrive home earlier than they said they would. After all, his mom said they'd be home *by* 9:30, not *at* 9:30.

As Jason finally approached the back roads leading into his neighborhood, he attempted to formulate a story in his head on why he was out in case his parents were home. However, coming up with excuses was next to impossible as his mind kept focusing on *really* hoping his parents were not home yet so he didn't have to say anything. As he turned the corner and made his way down his street, he saw that his house was still dark which provided much-needed relief. He sped into the driveway, skidded to a halt, punched the garage door code into the keypad, and looked around as the garage door rose. His pulse raced and he was breathing so hard that, for a moment, he thought he might pass out in the garage.

He placed his bike and helmet back exactly where they were about two hours ago and ran inside. He turned on a bunch of lights and ran up to his room. He stripped off his water and sweat-soaked clothes, grabbed his towel, and got into the shower. As the water ran down on him and his pulse finally began returning to normal, he couldn't help but think back to where he just was. The water coming out of the store's sprinkler system was icy cold whereas the water in this shower was perfect.

Jason turned off the water and stepped out of the shower. He put on some clean clothes and carried his wet clothes down to the laundry room. Just as he started the washer, he heard the garage door rise. *I did it,* he thought to himself as his shoulders dropped from a huge exhale. *Just play it cool.*

The door opened and his mom walked in. Jason strode up from the basement and met her at the top of the stairs.

"Hi, honey. How was your night?" said his mom, who seemed a little tipsy; not too uncommon after a night out with friends.

"It was fine. Just watched some TV. How was dinner?" said Jason.

"Oh, it was good. Sorry we're late, there was something going on at the mall."

"Yeah, it was a fire." Jason's body immediately tensed.

Jason's dad, John, appeared and looked at him, "How do you know that?"

Jason's stomach clenched, and he tried not to panic. "I ... heard it on the radio." Jason lied for the third time tonight.

"The radio?" asked John.

"Yeah, some caller called in and mentioned that she saw a bunch of fire trucks at the mall." Jason knew this wasn't his best response. The radio? Seriously?

"That makes sense. It was a mess, and we had to take the long way home," said Debbie.

"It's no big deal. Also, Gregg went out earlier with some friends."

"Okay. Did you take the chicken out of the freezer like I asked?"

Jason tilted his head back and slapped his hand on his forehead. "I'll get it now."

Jason went back down to the basement and smiled as the remaining wave of relief washed over him.

17.

LORI TOOK HER TIME GETTING HOME. HER MOM KNEW SHE WAS OUT WITH friends so there was no rush although the thin handles from the Southpoint shopping bag digging into her wrist was enough of an annoyance, and a reminder, that the sooner she got home, the better. She was not proud of what she did but sometimes the invisible pull of doing the right thing, even if that thing wasn't totally clear yet, was impossible to ignore.

She took the headsets that they were using, the Red Chip, some cables, and the user manual. She's fairly confident that Pete would not rat them out. She also couldn't help but think that Pete almost wanted them to take this stuff based on his support for Jason after hearing the story and despite the chaotic environment they were just in. That was what Lori was going to tell herself anyway, at least, when she needed a smidge of justification for her outright theft.

After dumping her bike and helmet in the garage, Lori went inside to where her mom, Paula, and sister, Stephanie, were watching a movie together in the den. Lori was glad the three of them got to stay in the house and not move because of the divorce. If anything, the house had been a source of unspoken comfort for Lori and Stephanie even though they would not have any future memories there with their father. Lori, Stephanie, and Paula had become much closer over the last two years, something Paula was particularly grateful for, considering how impressionable kids were at fifteen and ten. Her biggest fear was, and continued to be, that her kids would become bitter over the divorce. As of now, that didn't seem to be the case; although, one never knew with divorce. The one, slight upside was that there were other kids at their respective schools (and in general) whose parents had divorced or separated, and her kids might find some comfort in that.

Lori said hello but went straight to her bedroom to hide the shopping bag in her closet before going back to answer all of her mom's questions about how her night was.

A few minutes later, she reappeared as the movie was ending.

"How was your night?" asked Paula.

"It was fine. I just met up with some friends. We didn't do much," said Lori.

Stephanie was lying on the couch with one leg draped over the armrest fumbling through the regular channels on the television when Paula looked over and called out, "Go back a sec, Steph."

"What? It's just the news," said Stephanie.

"I know but ... will you just turn it back for a minute, please?"

Stephanie switched the channels back to the local news where a news anchor was now standing very close to where Jason and Lori were only about forty-five minutes ago, reporting on the fire.

"Looks like a fire at the mall. I'm glad you weren't there," said Paula.

"Oh, wow," said Lori in what she hoped was enough of a disinterested tone to not attract her mom's glance. "Doesn't look too bad, thankfully."

"Yeah, I guess not."

Lori then remembered Pete. She was supposed to text him when they got home. Not only that, but she was now wondering if Pete also got out okay.

"Can I change this now?" said Stephanie.

"Yeah, go ahead. I was just curious what that was."

After a few more minutes of watching split seconds of dozens of channels, courtesy of Stephanie, Lori yawned and got up. "I'm going to bed. I'll see you in the morning."

"Everything okay, sweetie?" said Paula.

"Yep. Just tired. Good night."

"Good night."

Stephanie said nothing and just continued staring at the television in a trance.

After showering, Lori went into her room and did, in fact, get ready for bed. She turned out all the lights except for her desk lamp. She sat at her desk and pulled out her phone to text Pete.

Hey it's Lori. We're both home. U ok?

She then went into her closet and retrieved the manual. She sat at her desk and kept a small stack of papers nearby in case her mom or Stephanie walked in uninvited. She would easily be able to hide the thin booklet without making it obvious. Not that they would look that closely, but as a rookie thief, Lori's paranoia was pretty high at the moment.

Lori noticed that this was not a typical user manual filled with warnings and other boring mumbo jumbo in multiple languages. Instead, this was printed in easy to understand wording that spelled out exactly how the system worked. There was a unique website and several codes that needed to be entered followed by a cell phone number that was verified. After that, the prompts on the screen would do most of the work for the user. Lori still harbored a healthy dose of skepticism about the whole thing, but she had come this far; the headsets were literally sitting in her closet, and needed to see this through.

Her phone then chimed and Pete's number came up.

Yep. We left about 5 min after you. They made us leave. We were SOAKED LOL. It's a mess but whatever. I don't think the fire was 2 bad.

Lori smiled and wrote back.

Ok glad ur ok. Good night.

Before turning in for the night, she decided to write an email to Jason to come clean about what she took from

Southfield's. He probably figured it out, but just in case he didn't. Also, if they were going to test these out, they would need to do it sooner rather than later. She opened her laptop and waited for everything to boot up.

Jason sat in his room, still somewhat amazed that he got away with his mall adventure. He opened his laptop to see if Lori got home all right. He was not supposed to be using his laptop either, but his parents didn't bother to take it away, like they did his phone, because he needs it for school.

He opened the chat window and after about fifteen minutes saw Lori's name appear.

> Jason: Hey…you home ok?
>
> Lori: Yeah. How about you? Did you get busted?
>
> Jason: No – made it with a few minutes to spare. The traffic slowed my parents down.
>
> Lori: Cool! Can I come by tomorrow?
>
> Jason: Should be ok. I'll just tell my parents we have to study for that bio test we have next Friday. Everything ok?
>
> Lori: Yep, all good. I'll bring my science books.
>
> Jason: OK. Hey, what was in the shopping bag?
>
> Lori: I gotta go. TTYL.
>
> Jason: Wait!

Lori signed off the chat and sat up in bed, her laptop still open on her lap, staring straight ahead. She was in the class when Jason and Trevor got caught, but she didn't witness the tire incident. She knew, though, her friend would never do something like that. In fact, Lori didn't even believe that Jason knew *how* to let the air out of a tire, much less orchestrate a plan to do so.

Lori was suddenly exhausted, the adrenaline long gone. All she wanted to do now was sleep, but decided to send the email.

To: Jason

Subject: Top Secret!

Hey Jason,

I took the two headsets and the other things Pete mentioned when we left the mall earlier tonight. Please don't say anything. I don't know what came over me, I just felt like...when the alarms were going off and we had to run, I had to make a split decision and I grabbed them.

I just finished skimming the user manual. The Look-Back feature actually seems pretty interesting and is surprisingly easy to use. I'll read it again tomorrow morning. I haven't used the headset yet to see if it works (probably not) but I'll bring it all over. Anyway, here are some of the highlights so we don't have to spend too much time discussing it in a whisper.

1. Without the chip, there's like 100 different places to choose from. Each time you go to a place, it's the same. So, if we went back to the World Trade Center tomorrow, it would be the same exact thing that we saw earlier today. I think Pete mentioned this as well...can't remember.

2. Everything changes once you insert the Red Chip. We need to download a program from a special website and enter in a bunch of codes and a phone number.

3. Then, a calendar appears with the last date being whatever yesterday was. So, if it's October 1st today, you can go back to a window of time from Sept 1st to Sept 30th.

4. The program says something about a 20-mile max radius. That's the maximum distance we can wander out. Since we both had our phones in school, we should be fine.

5. We then set the location and the time of day and then there is a countdown. After that I'm not sure. I'm assuming (hoping) it's awesome though. We'll find out.

6. One feature that sounds amazing is that we can take still images of whatever we see at any point. Those images can then be sent to a phone or email. Crazy right? I'll explain how to take the pictures when I see you.

I'm beat. I'm going to sleep now- Thanks for taking me with you tonight. Even though it was bizarre, I feel like we were supposed to discover this technology. I'm delirious.

Goodnight. –L

Lori closed her laptop, laid back on her bed, and immediately fell asleep.

18.
Southfield's, 11:37 p.m.

THE FIRE ALARMS AND SPRINKLERS LASTED FOR ABOUT FIFTEEN MINUTES causing hundreds of thousands of dollars worth of damage. The irony of the whole thing was that the *actual* fire only caused a few hundred dollars in damage. The fire was contained within a very small section on the first floor and was extinguished by some staff members relatively quickly. Why all the sprinklers went off in the department store was anyone's guess, but it was safe to assume that there would be plenty of finger pointing over the next few months as people tried to understand who would pay for the extensive damage.

Both levels of the mall looked like a war zone. There was water everywhere. The tiled aisles became as slick as ice rinks. Clothes on hangers looked like wet towels, and there were beads of water dripping from the winter coats into newly formed puddles on the thin carpet directly underneath. Water continued to trickle down both the walls and the mirrored columns, and there was a haze of steam rising toward the ceiling where it remained. Shattered glass lay on the ground near some display cases that either caved in or were somehow destroyed by all the chaos and confusion.

Two hours after the alarms were turned off, employees were allowed back inside. Most of the mall employees went straight home as it was initially unknown how long they would need to stay away. Southfield's managers, however, waited it out nearby and promptly returned to the store when they were alerted that it was safe to do so.

After receiving Pete's call about what happened, Steve sent Pete and the others home. He was now the electronics department employee in charge of looking over the inventory.

The general reaction was complete shock when these employees returned to the department store. Primarily, though, people were just confused, and simply did not know what to do or where to begin in terms of the clean-up. Several fire and police personnel were walking around checking different sections of the store. Since every fire sprinkler went off, the entire store needed to be canvassed and determined to be safe before the cleaning crew could enter the building.

The employees were brought to a central location on the first floor where a couple of official looking people got up on a make-shift stage. The stage was hastily put together with cinderblocks and plywood. A woman in a fluorescent green t-shirt with a walkie-talkie on her belt stepped forward and spoke into a bullhorn.

"Ladies and gentlemen, I'm going to be brief as it's very late and we want all of you to head home as quickly as possible. First, thank you for being here. As you can see, the fire that occurred earlier this evening triggered all the fire sprinklers to engage, which has caused quite a mess to say the least. We are committed to getting this facility fully restored in a matter of days. Beginning tomorrow morning at 6:00 a.m., cleaning crews will arrive to begin the process of removing the water, broken glass, and any merchandise that cannot be salvaged. What we need from all of you is to head to your departments and secure any small merchandise that may still be outstanding. This includes jewelry, electronics, home goods, et cetera. As you can see, many items will not need to be secured as they are completely destroyed. Again, all we're asking is that you lock up the smaller items so the cleaning crews can do their jobs quickly and efficiently. Once you have these items locked up, please head home. Finally, if you see anything suspicious, notify one of our representatives who will be walking around. They are wearing the same green t-shirt that I have on and will take your information to expedite the process. We will contact you with our plan for re-opening as soon as we can. Thank you again for your help tonight."

The crowd gradually began to talk and then dispersed to their respective departments.

Steve headed up to the second floor to survey the damage. As he walked by many of the flat screen televisions, he easily saw that the ones on display were now waterlogged and worthless. The televisions that were still in the boxes may be salvageable. The outsides of the boxes were wet but the water may not have penetrated through to the televisions themselves. The worst case for those sets would probably be marking the price way down, so they could be sold and moved off the floor quickly.

As Steve walked around the corner, he noticed that the display case that showcased both Collins VR headsets was opened, and both headsets were missing. He looked around the immediate area and saw no trace of them. He pulled out his phone and called Pete.

Pete was at home reading a *PCMag* on his bed and, although it was late, was nowhere near ready for sleep.

"Hey, Steve," answered Pete.

"Hey, Pete. Sorry to bother you. Where are the two headsets that were in the case? It's empty," said Steve.

"I was showing them to a potential customer when the sprinklers and alarms went off. They should be under the cash register in the cabinet."

Steve turned and looked at the register that was covered with a tarp.

"Okay, hang on a sec. Sorry again for the late call. You should see what this place looks like." Steve opened the cabinet, crouched down, and peered inside. "There's nothing here, Pete," said Steve.

"Are you sure?"

"Yes, I'm sure. I see some extra shopping bags, papers, and the wires from the cash register. No headsets. They're gone."

"I don't know what to say."

"Pete, tell me you didn't take these."

"I didn't take the headsets."

"You know if you did, that would be—"

"Hey, I didn't take them all right? Check the security cameras."

"The cameras are likely destroyed."

Pete rolled his eyes. "The footage, Steve. Not the actual cameras."

Steve sighed, realizing his mistake. "I swear, my brain is like mush right now."

Pete took a breath and calmly stated, "Steve, I did nothing wrong. There was chaos and confusion. I was showing the headsets to a couple of kids, and I asked them to place the headsets under the cabinet before we all had to evacuate. They were helping me out while the water was raining down and destroying all the merchandise. We didn't have a lot of time for planning."

Steve was silent for a moment. "So, the kids stole the headsets? What are their names?"

"Whoa. I just said they put the headsets under the cabinet. I don't know why they would take the headsets, and I definitely didn't see them steal anything."

Steve stared at the empty cabinet. He didn't have the energy to argue; he would have to take matters into his own hands.

"Okay, fine. I'll be in touch when I know more about the reopening."

"Any idea how long that will be?"

"None." Steve hung up his phone.

A few minutes later, Steve spotted one of the people in a green t–shirt, raised his hand, and screamed across the floor, "Hey, you! I got property missing."

The man in the green t-shirt put up one finger to signal to Steve that he heard him, but he needed to finish up with someone in the furniture department first.

Steve sarcastically thought to himself, *Right, because I'm sure someone walked out with a loveseat during all the confusion.*

Ten minutes later, the man appeared.

"Hi, sir. I'm Rich. How can I help?"

"I have two virtual reality headsets missing. My employee took them out of a display case before the chaos started."

"Okay, I understand. I just need to get some information from you, and we'll file the report. What is the approximate dollar value of each item?" Rich listened intently, holding a pen to his clipboard, ready to take notes.

"About two-fifty."

"Wow. I didn't think those cost that much."

"Are you accusing me of lying?"

"No, no, of course not. I just feel like I've seen them much cheaper elsewhere."

"You probably have. But these are better. They have features that the cheaper models don't have." Steve instinctively went into sales mode.

"I see. Any accessories taken along with them?"

"Yeah, some cables which leads me to believe that this was deliberate and not a mistake."

Steve then remembered the Red Chip and the manual that he had hid in the cabinet earlier in the day, causing his anxiety to go up another fifty notches. He now needed Rich out of the picture before he could look for those items.

"I see. So, you can't really use the headsets without the cables and the cables by themselves are—"

"What?" said Steve, rejoining the conversation. "Uh, worthless, yes."

"Got it. What is the value of the cables?"

"Not sure. They come with the headsets," said Steve, staring at the cabinet door.

"Oh, I see. No problem. I'll just add them to the list. Anything else?"

"Well, we definitely have some damaged televisions and laptops that were on display. Additionally, I'm not sure if water penetrated the television boxes that are out on the floor over there." Steve pointed in the general direction of the TVs.

"I understand. We'll have a separate team inspect all of those over the next few days. I'm just here to see if anything was physically missing like the headsets you described."

Steve refocused on Rich. "I see. I'm sure there will be more paperwork needed. Do you need anything else from me regarding these? I'd like to get out of here."

"No sir. You're all set. I appreciate you alerting me. Take care." Rich walked away.

Just as Rich was out of sight, Steve knelt back down and rifled through the papers in the cabinet. He immediately started to sweat and shake when he realized that both the black box containing the Red Chip and the manual were gone. He ran his hands through his hair over and over again and started to bite his thumb nail as he paced in circles. He took a few deep breaths and tried to calm himself down as he walked out of the mall. He realized that figuring out who took the sensitive merchandise was out of his control at the moment but, as Pete said, the security footage could hopefully save him from receiving any of the blame himself.

19.

Sunday

STEVE DIDN'T SLEEP MUCH DESPITE IT BEING A WEEKEND NIGHT AND NOW having a few days off while Southfield's was cleaned from top to bottom. He got out of bed, so as not to disturb his wife, and went down to the kitchen to make some coffee and figure out a story for Ted. Ted wouldn't care about the headsets since those were covered under insurance, but the Red Chip—that Steve was never supposed to have—would be a whole different story.

Steve grabbed a notepad and a pen from the drawer, sat down at his kitchen table and started to think. There wasn't much to write, but he thought better with a pen in his hand for some reason. He thought to himself, *I could say that the package arrived and then the contents were stolen. That could work but that would also lead Ted to ask me why I didn't alert him immediately. Ted can spot liars like no one I've ever seen. On the other hand, I could put the blame on Pete since he did sign for it after all. But that wouldn't work either since Pete told me about the items right away.* Steve took a sip of his coffee. *On the third hand, I could blame Ted since it's his product. I mean, I only heard about all of this yesterday.* He tapped his chin with the pen and took a deep breath. *Then again, blaming Ted is like throwing gasoline on a bonfire.* Steve continued to think while he drank his coffee. After about ten minutes, he decided it was best to come clean and hope Ted would not completely lose his mind.

Steve looked at the clock and his eyes got heavy, despite the coffee. He would call Jane in a few hours to let her know the situation. This way he avoided an initial, direct conversation with Ted and would appear to be doing the right thing because he was up late taking care of Collins's other merchandise at Southfield's. Perfect.

20.

REED'S COFFEE SHOP, A POPULAR SPOT IN THE MIDDLE OF OAK BROOK, hummed with activity as its customers met with friends or worked away on their laptops while drinking coffee and eating pastries. Reed's was also Roger Hagen's favorite place to spend Sunday mornings, so he decided that this would be a good location to set up a meeting with Ted Collins to talk about the episode involving his son, Trevor, and Jason Markum.

Ted's influence on the school, and the town in general, was, unfortunately, rather significant. As far as this principal was concerned, Roger has already found himself considering changes based solely on Ted's "recommendations." For instance, there was the floated idea of not penalizing students who come into school late in the mornings since "some students are simply not morning people." There was also the ridiculous suggestion of parents (Ted) reviewing their children's grades prior to them being sent out in formal report cards "just in case the teachers made a mistake."

The bottom line for Roger was that if he really wanted to change the quickly forming perception of him being a pushover in Ted's eyes, he needed to get tougher. Roger also knew that Trevor was very likely involved in, if not solely responsible for, "The Incident," but without proof, could not simply blame him. Instead, he wanted to discuss a possible compromise so that the students were aware that behavior like that would not be tolerated, and the parents and teachers were aware that Roger, not Ted, was the one in charge of Parker High School.

Ted walked into the coffee shop and removed his sunglasses. He spotted Roger near the window and walked over to him.

"Ted, thank you for coming. I tried calling you all week," said Roger putting his phone on the table and rising out of his seat to shake hands.

"It's all right. Busy week. What's this about?" said Ted, shaking Roger's hand and then sitting down.

"Well, I'll get right to it. Your son and another student were found together looking through quiz scores in class and then later in the teachers' parking lot, where apparently one or both of them let the air out of Mrs. Goldfeather's tires."

"Who?" asked Ted.

"Mrs. Gold—their biology teacher."

Ted stared at Roger seemingly wanting to hear more. "That's it?"

"Um, yes, that's it. It's a serious violation of our honor code, not to mention vandalism, and we cannot let this incident go unpunished."

Ted smirked and said, "Look, Roger, I just got word that some important products of mine disappeared recently, and

I'm a little distracted. Let's get right to it. Did Trevor physically harm anyone?"

"Not that I'm aware of but, as I said, he and another student—"

"It wasn't Trevor."

"Well, that's still unclear. Both students have blamed each other."

"Of course, they have. Who's the other student?"

"Jason Markum."

"Ha! I know him. I wouldn't put it past him to do something like this."

Roger furrowed his brow. "Why would you—"

"Roger, my son did not do this. He may have been there, for whatever reason, but he's not a savage. Our family does not let the air out of tires or vandalize anything, *ever*! Do I make myself clear?"

"I understand, but—"

"Additionally," said Ted, leaning closer and lowering his voice, "I don't I think I need to remind you that the Board of Education, who, if I'm not mistaken, needs to decide soon on whether to extend your contract for next year. You signed on only for a year initially. Am I correct?"

This was the other side of Ted Collins that only a few people, outside of his company, ever saw. A bully who used his wealth and authority to get his way and get himself or his family out of tough situations.

Roger Hagen, taken aback by what Ted just said, yet also unsure whether to rise up or not at this point in the conversation, slumped his shoulders slightly and muttered,

"Yes, you're correct. My contract is, in fact, already up for renewal during this probationary period."

"Well, I think you've done a fine job here over the last few months and I'd like to see you in your position a little longer."

"That's nice of you to say."

"Don't mention it," said Ted, now looking around. "I think this meeting is resolved, don't you?"

"Yes, it is. For the record, I never did think your son would do something like this. I just needed to respond professionally since he was there during the incidents," said Roger, mentally kicking himself for, once again, caving in to Ted's intimidation.

"I understand, Principal."

"Well, once again, I appreciate you coming here to discuss this matter face to face," said Roger, slowly rising out of his seat.

Ted put up his hand. "There is one more thing, Roger."

Roger sat back down, surprised. "What's that?"

"I think there's enough here to suspend Jason Markum."

Roger's face indicated confusion at Ted's latest request. "Well ... we'll need to confirm—"

"You heard me. That kid is bad news."

"I wouldn't go that far."

"Well, I would. And I am. Trevor says that he's a very negative person and, after this incident, told me he thinks he's mentally unstable as well."

Unknowingly, Ted just gave Roger one more chance to show some guts and take control of this situation. Roger took a sip of his coffee, his hand shaking slightly, and said, "Hang on a minute. You asked me a second ago who the other student involved was."

"And?"

"And you just said that Trevor said Jason is mentally unstable after the incident."

"I'm not following you."

"Ted, I asked you here to *tell* you about what happened. If you already knew about it, then why did you act surprised when I told you that the other student was Jason Markum?"

"Don't twist this around Roger. I'm really not in the mood today."

"No, I just—"

"I don't want any of this getting out about my son, okay?" Ted took a breath and then said in a more measured tone, "However, we both know that we can't just sweep this under the rug because the other teachers will get suspicious. I get that. So, suspend Jason, and let's move on."

"I'm sorry but I cannot just suspend a student without cause."

"You have cause!" yelled Ted while banging the table with his fist. His impatience quickly rising to the surface. This drew stares from the customers sitting nearby. Then, quieter, "Roger. A teacher's tires were flattened for God's sake. Every parent is already aware."

Roger, looking around nervously, responded, "Yes, I realize that, but we have no *proof.* He said/he said isn't enough. We can open the school up to a potential lawsuit, not to mention a ton of criticism."

Ted waved his arm as if swatting flies away from his face. "Nonsense, I have plenty of lawyers who can protect the school. Suspend the kid, and you'll be principal for as long as you want. Don't, and you're done."

Roger was stunned at what he just heard. "That's blackmail, Ted."

Ted stared Roger down. "Be careful with your words, Roger. My concern is with my son and our family's reputation. I expect this to be taken care of in the next week."

Ted stood, took a twenty-dollar bill out of his wallet and dropped it on the table.

"Coffee's on me," said Ted, as he walked out of the coffee shop.

Roger sat silently, speechless at what Ted had just said to him. After a few minutes, he removed earbuds from his bag, fitted them into his ears, plugged the other end into his phone, and thought more about this entire situation which had just become a lot more complicated.

21.

PRIOR TO LEAVING REED'S PARKING LOT, TED CALLED JANE FROM HIS CAR to discuss the missing Red Chip in more detail. She reiterated what she sent him in an email which was what Steve had explained to her a couple hours earlier. The items were sent to Southfield's by mistake and now they were missing. Ted asked her to set up an emergency meeting for later that day to get to the bottom of the situation. Those items needed to be found immediately.

Ted knew he was playing with fire by moving forward with this technology for the public, but it was an opportunity that he simply could not pass up. To succeed in business, his father taught him, you must spot the opportunities and act on them before anyone else does. In his mind, this technology could be the biggest innovation since the television, and there was no way he was going to sit idly by.

As Ted put his car into reverse, another SUV, all black with blacked out windows, pulled up sideways behind his car. Ted did not see the car at first and continued to back up until he lightly struck the SUV's passenger door behind him. He then looked in his rearview mirror and cursed while smashing his hand down on the steering wheel. He pulled forward, put his car in park, got out, and walked toward the driver's window.

"What the hell are you doing?" yelled Ted with his arms in the air.

The driver sat motionless in the car, and then the rear doors opened. Two men appeared. They looked familiar, but Ted couldn't place them. They instructed him to get back into his car and unlock the doors.

"What is this?" demanded Ted.

One of the men pulled out a Taser, and Ted immediately recognized it from the Valhalla lab. He quickly put the pieces together. *They* wanted to talk with him—in broad daylight.

"Sir, we can do this the easy way or my way. Get back in your car and let us in." It was the same guy who had checked his I.D. at the Valhalla gate a few months ago.

Ted knew there was no easy way out of this situation, so he backtracked to his car and unlocked the doors.

"Sir, are you all right?" said a coffee shop patron as he left the store. "Do you need help?"

Ted, looking back with a fake smile, replied, "Everything's fine. Thank you. Just some friends."

The man in the black sunglasses then said to Ted, "Let's go. In the car and drive to your office, now. No stopping. Any nonsense and we'll head to your house instead. Got it?"

"I got it. I got it. You won't need those," nodding toward the tasers.

After about fifteen minutes, both SUVs arrived at Collins Industries. As they approached the guard house, they came upon the one employee who was on the grounds. No one worked on Sundays, not even the company's internal security guards, since the office was filled with motion detectors and cameras. One of the benefits of being in the electronics business was the cost savings of needing actual personnel for certain positions, like security.

Ted rolled down the window and smiled at the man in the booth.

"Hi there. I'm just showing some friends the place. We won't be too long."

The guard smiled back. "Not a problem, Mr. Collins. Go right ahead." The guard opened the gate, waved the cars through, closed the door, and resumed reading his magazine. The SUVs continued through the wooded drive to the main building, set back about a quarter of a mile. They parked in the first two parking spaces directly in front of the building's main entrance.

Samantha and the two female guards from Valhalla emerged from the SUV while the two men escorted Ted out of his own car. Ted looked at the five of them all dressed in black and said sarcastically, "You know, all of you dressed like ninjas has the opposite effect of appearing to blend in around here."

Samantha stepped forward in front of Ted and slapped him across the face with her black-gloved right hand. The two female guards sneered at Ted as they stood behind Samantha, no doubt enjoying this. Samantha removed her gloves and put them in her back pocket and stared right at Ted.

"Who is Pete Davis, Mr. Collins?" said Samantha.

"Wha— Who?" said Ted, stunned, his face stinging from the smack.

"Pete. Davis," repeated Samantha.

"How the hell should I know?" barked Ted.

Samantha slapped Ted again, this time with her bare left hand. Ted didn't even have a chance to flinch before her hand crossed his face. In the instant it took Ted to move ever so slightly in Samantha's direction, the two guards seized Ted's arms and held him still.

"We have all day, Ted. No one's coming to save you," Samantha continued in a steady tone of voice. In fact, did you even recognize the guard at the gate?"

"No, actually," replied Ted through clenched teeth. His face felt like it was on fire.

"I know you didn't. He works for us." Samantha let that one sink in for a moment. "Now, again, does Pete Davis work for you?"

"Samantha, I'm telling you, I don't know a Pete Davis. Can you give me more information? I realize I'm not in a position to lie right now."

Samantha nodded at the guards to let Ted's arms go. Samantha was in control here and she knew that if Ted so much as sneezed in her direction, his next breath would be a painful one.

"Yesterday, in the early afternoon, a high school student by the name of Pete Davis logged into the system from Southfield's department store. The only way that interface is accessible is by having the knowledge and/or the manual that has the directions and passwords and by having a Red Chip. You gave us all your Red Chips did you not?"

"Yes, I gave you two of them."

"There are others?"

"Of course, there are others. We typically develop multiple prototypes at one time so we can do various tests to isolate and then correct issues. It's common practice." Ted knew this answer might earn him another slap but couldn't lie.

"I see. I seem to recall you specifically telling me that we had what you produced and that there were no others when we spoke three months ago."

"It wasn't intentional to keep some from you. Whether I gave you all of the prototypes at the time you asked for them wouldn't have mattered as we can always produce more." Ted was really testing the waters here.

"And why would you produce more, Ted?" Samantha's patience was running out.

Ted shifted slightly causing the guards to stir and replied, "I'm not saying we would produce more. I'm saying we *could*. We still have the blueprints for the work done up to that point."

That last answer also toed the line of truth, and Ted was hoping that Samantha wouldn't pick up on it.

"I see. We commissioned your company to build these chips for us. These are not for anyone else, and I don't think I need to tell you why."

"Actually, I don't know what these are for," said Ted. "No one's ever told me. Regarding the outstanding chips, I'll be sure and speak with my team about it."

"That's a good start. Then, you will personally destroy the rest and hand them over so we know the job is done. And Ted? I'm not asking."

Ted almost rolled his eyes but caught himself. "Let me just smash them to pieces. I really don't need another visit from you and your goons about this, Samantha."

Samantha stared at him and Ted steadied himself in case another swat was on the way. Instead, she said, "No. I want evidence of the destroyed chips. Get your keys out."

"Sorry?"

"We're going up to your office."

Samantha didn't wait for a response and began walking to the building's main entrance. The two female guards followed her while the other two men stared at Ted until he headed toward the main doors.

Once they were in front of the glass doors, Ted searched on his key ring, found the correct key, and unlocked the door. In the vestibule, he deactivated the beeping alarm panel and then continued on into the main lobby. Samantha and her crew followed Ted up an open staircase to the second floor and then down a carpeted hallway until they reached his office door. Ted took out the key ring again, found the correct key to his office, unlocked the door, and walked inside.

He turned on the lights and then moved farther in when he said, "Okay, Samantha. Why are we here?"

Samantha looked around the spacious office and noticed the bookshelves lined with books, expensive paintings on the wall, several windows looking out over the wooded area around the building, and then finally what she hoped to see. She looked over and nodded to one of the females who walked behind Ted's desk and picked up the framed family portrait and brought it around.

"Um, excuse me? Please, don't touch my things," said Ted.

The guard ignored Ted and handed the frame to Samantha who grabbed it with her now gloved hands.

"Lovely family, Ted. Is it just your wife and one son?"

Ted sighed. "Yeah."

Samantha handed the frame back to the guard and nodded. The guard walked over to a small table in Ted's office and proceeded to remove the photo from the frame. She then handed the photo to Samantha who folded it in half and placed it in her back pocket.

Samantha walked right in front of Ted's face and said, "You have one final chance to hand over all remaining Red Chips. If another notification comes up in our labs about this rogue Red Chip, we're going to have a real problem, Ted. This technology is important for reasons that you'll never fully understand, and we cannot have it compromised by anyone."

"I understand," said Ted, realizing he had no way out of this.

"Good. I hope, for your sake, this is our last discussion." Samantha nodded at the four guards and they all filed out of his office and back down the main staircase. They walked outside into their black SUV and drove away leaving Ted standing in his office staring at the empty picture frame.

22.

AROUND THE SAME TIME SAMANTHA WAS USING TED'S FACE AS A punching bag, Lori was riding her bike over to Jason's house.

Jason's mom answered the door. "Hi, Lori. How're you doing?"

"Hi, Mrs. Markum. I'm doing well. How are you?" said Lori.

"I'm just fine, thanks for asking. Come on in. Jason told me you guys have a big test next week?" said Debbie, waving her in and smiling.

"Yeah, biology on Friday." Lori walked into the foyer. "We figured we might as well start studying now. Mrs. Goldfeather's tests are never easy."

"Well, it's good you're here. Go ahead upstairs and help yourselves to a snack whenever you guys are hungry."

"Thanks, Mrs. Markum."

Lori walked up to Jason's room and emptied the contents of her backpack onto his bed. The room was decorated very simply with some knick-knacks from when Jason was younger. Gold, plastic trophies from little league still held space on the higher shelves while the lower shelves housed several middle-grade book series. The beige walls and light blue carpet were only noticeable if you were paying attention, although the lack of pictures of any kind–even a cheesy sports or car poster or two–zapped the room of any real personality.

A minute later, Jason walked into his room and stared at what Lori had put on his bed.

"Shut the door," said Lori, looking up.

Jason shut the door without taking his eyes off his bed.

"Lock it."

Jason locked the door, although it was just a puny door knob lock and not a deadbolt. It really couldn't keep anyone out.

"I can't believe these are in here," said Jason, looking at the two pairs of headsets they used the night before.

Lori smiled. "When we were helping Pete put the stuff away, I found myself under the tarp and it was just an impulse. I've never stolen anything before. Ever."

"I knew there was something important in the bag, but I didn't think it would be these. You can get in a ton of trouble if someone catches you."

"I know but there was so much chaos in the store, I knew I could get away with it. When we walked through the emergency exit, there wasn't even a security scanner like they have in the main entrance. Also, everyone had shopping bags, so I didn't look out of place."

"We need to bring these headsets back."

"I know."

"Like, right now." Jason's expression was that of dead seriousness.

"Hang on," said Lori, putting up her hand. "Why don't we set them up and see what else they can do? I promise to get them back to the store immediately after."

Jason shifted nervously while continuing to stare at everything on his bed. "I don't know. It doesn't feel right to me. I mean, I read your email, but this seems wrong."

"*You* didn't do anything wrong. If I get in trouble, I'll just tell them that I brought them over here without you knowing. I'll take the fall."

Jason contorted his face slightly. "Why do you want to risk getting in trouble? I mean, you would be in, like, police trouble."

"Because your situation with Trevor really sucks, that's why. That kid is a bully and I'm tired of seeing him always get his way."

"Yeah, I know, but his issue is with me, not you. Why do you want to get back at him so bad?"

Lori looked away and her voice caught in her throat. "I shouldn't say," she answered in a low tone.

"Are you okay?" Jason asked, now worried that he said something terrible. "Listen, I appreciate your help and the fact that you even went this far for me. I just don't want to see you get in worse trouble for it."

Lori was silent for several seconds and then pulled out Jason's desk chair and sat down. "Can I tell you something?"

Jason sat on his bed. "Yeah, of course. What's up?"

"No, I mean you *cannot* repeat this. It's incredibly personal and I've never told anyone."

"I won't say a word, I promise," Jason said, raising his hand to his heart.

The mood in Jason's room became much heavier. Lori sat quietly for a few moments and took a deep breath.

"You know how my parents divorced two years ago, right?"

"Yeah, I remember you first telling me around our spring break in eighth grade."

"Yeah. Well, I never told you, or anyone, *why* they divorced."

"I know. I never asked either. It didn't seem right. My parents said the same thing to me at the time. They said it would be rude to ask such a personal question and that even though you're a friend, it's up to you to tell me. I knew it bothered you but that's why I never said anything."

Lori smiled a little. "I'm not mad or anything. I mean, even if you asked, I wouldn't have told you. Your parents do know, by the way. They've actually been really supportive to my mom and me over the last two years."

Jason was a little confused at this news, not because it wasn't great to hear his parents stepped up, but because he truly had no idea any of this went on. He then looked at Lori and said, "Lori, what exactly happened?"

Lori took a mini breath. "Trevor's parents had a Christmas party that year. I guess they have one every year, and my mom was out of town, but she said that my dad should go as it was nice of the Collins's to invite them. So, he went. Well, while he was there, Trevor's mom apparently introduced one of her single friends to my dad at that party. According to my dad, it was just a polite gesture since he didn't know too many people at the party. In fact, I guess your parents weren't there?"

"Probably not. I would've remembered. Anyway, continue."

"The whole thing has never sat right with me. I think Trevor's mom was more concerned with trying to find her friend a new boyfriend and where that man came from, even if it meant a man from another family in the same town, was irrelevant to her. I've said this to my mom a couple of different times, but she always dismisses me. She says it's a pretty mean accusation to make, although I'm still not convinced. There are other things, too."

"What do you mean?" said Jason, trying to process what he was hearing.

"There has not been one time, not one single time, where Trevor's mom expressed any type of sympathy or concern that my parents were divorcing. There were plenty of times she could have said something to me, even in private, but chose not to. Last spring, we were at one of my softball games and my dad and his now new wife, the *same* woman from that party, were there, sitting on the opposite side from my mom. My mom could clearly see Trevor's mom parading my dad and his new wife around, introducing them to people and obviously taking credit for bringing them together. Of course, she would need to be involved. It was never any secret where Trevor developed that part of his charming personality from. I know it was killing my mom but she put on a brave face and sat there, ignoring the stares from the other parents."

Jason looked down and said nothing. He, of course, never knew any of this and never suspected it either. Why would he? This type of drama, real or imagined, had not yet entered his life, and he certainly wasn't seeking it out.

In that moment, though, he had a new respect for his friend and all she'd been through. Additionally, it now made more sense why she felt compelled to steal the headsets. It wasn't about the technology. It was about possibly getting back at a family who she felt damaged hers.

"I ... I don't know what to say. I'm so sorry to hear that and I won't say anything to anyone. I swear."

"I know you won't. That's why I told you. I've wanted to tell someone for a while." Lori took a deep breath and let out an exaggerated sigh.

"I have one question." Jason couldn't help himself.

"What's that?"

"Where was Trevor with all of this? I mean, was he even aware of ... how this all went down?"

Lori looked down and smoothed out her jeans. "I'm sure he was. It's just ... while he's never said anything directly to me, I've caught him, many times, giving me that annoying-as-hell smirk or whispering to his moron friends only to have them look over and grin in my direction." Lori was getting worked up but caught herself. "Okay, enough with the downer story. Are you ready to do this?" She smiled at Jason, and sensing it was now okay to do so, he smiled back.

"Yeah, let's give these a shot. Why not?"

"That's the spirit. Besides, just think about how great it'll be to get even with that loser using a product from his own father's company."

Jason thought about that for a moment and then smiled an even wider smile right back at Lori.

23.

THEY DECIDED TO USE LORI'S LAPTOP IN CASE JASON'S MOM CAME INTO HIS room. His mom would never go so far as to take someone else's laptop away. Also, if she asked what they were doing with the headsets, they would tell her that Lori got them as a gift and they were testing them out quickly before studying.

While Lori began setting up the program on her computer, Jason was opening each of their textbooks and scattering some biology notes around his room. Because of the flimsy lock on his door, these precautions were necessary.

For the next ten minutes, Lori sat at Jason's desk, alternating between looking at her laptop and the user manual and typing in different set up codes. She was nearly finished when Jason's mom knocked at the door, causing them both to jump.

"Hey, guys, do you want something to eat?" said Debbie through the door.

"Uh, not right now, mom. We'll come down later," said Jason.

"Okay, just checking."

Lori shook her head, smiled, and said, "Your mom's so cute."

A few minutes later, after one more computer restart, the program was ready for them to use.

"Okay, it's ready. One cable will connect my headset to the laptop and then we'll have a second cable connect my headset to your headset."

"Got it. Which one has the chip?"

"Mine does," said Lori, "It needs to connect directly to the computer. I say we test out another place first before we experiment with the time travel stuff. I'm a little nervous about jumping right into that."

"I dunno, I say we just do the Look-Back. We'll figure it out as we go," said Jason.

"I'm not so sure about that. Look, let's pick a new place first and really make sure this thing works. Okay?"

"Okay," Jason conceded.

"Where do you want to go?"

Jason shrugged. "I don't know. Where can we go?"

Lori smiled and swiveled around in the chair, facing the laptop again. A few seconds later, a full list of locations populated the screen, including:

The Taj Mahal
The South Pole
Hong Kong
The Eiffel Tower
Mexico City
Big Ben
The Golden Gate Bridge

Jason and Lori scanned the list to find a new location. Jason had already been to the World Trade Center twice.

Jason pointed to the screen and spoke up, "How about Niagara Falls?"

Lori, in a disinterested tone, responded, "Nah."

"The Alamo in Texas could be cool."

Lori ignored that one.

Jason then said, "Here it is."

Before he could say the name, Lori noticed what Jason was looking at and said, "Oh, yeah. That's perfect."

"All right, let's do this." Lori typed in a few more commands and pressed "Enter."

The instructions on the screen told them to put on their masks and make sure they were adjusted to fit snugly on their faces. Also on the computer screen was a counter in the bottom right-hand corner that began counting down from "30" when Lori pushed the Enter key a few seconds ago. As soon as the counter reached "10," both Lori and Jason saw the number "10" appear in their headsets followed by "9" as the seconds continued to count down.

As the counter reached "1," the screen went black and, just like when they were at the World Trade Center, it parted down the middle. They were now looking at the sign for The Night Train Roller Coaster at Summerland Amusement Park. They were standing outside of the building's entrance.

"Ready?" said Lori.

"Yeah, I guess. Let's point at the entrance and march."

They raised their arms and began walking into the building. After about a full minute of walking through a diffusely lit tunnel with thin, neon tube lights crisscrossing the walls and ceilings, Lori spoke up. "Dude, where's the ride?"

"It's up a little farther. It's a really popular ride. I was here two years ago. The line waiting to get in usually starts back outside. It sucks."

They continued on and finally entered a new room that had metal barricades that formed the waiting riders into an organized line. Despite it being empty, they still had to snake their way through the entire maze which actually enabled them to become pretty adept at turning and walking in the virtual world.

When they finally reached the safety gate and were next in line for the ride, the gate opened for them to proceed into the seats of the roller coaster. They walked deliberately toward the car and then they were automatically seated and buckled into place. A few moments later, the coaster took off. Jason and Lori remained standing in Jason's room.

The Night Train was an indoor roller coaster with laser lights and rock'n'roll music blasting the entire ride. The music today, though, was inaudible since there was no sound with the headsets, but the light shows and the very real feeling of riding the coaster was unbelievable. In fact, Lori had to sit down at one point and Jason had to grab onto his dresser as the ride was impacting their equilibriums and knocking them off-balance.

*

After riding The Night Train four times, Jason and Lori decided to end that session and call it a success. They were both pretty dizzy and even a little nauseous.

As Lori sat back down at the desk to reset the program on the laptop, Jason lay down on the carpet, staring at his ceiling with the backs of his hands resting on his forehead.

Lori swiveled around in the chair and looked down at Jason.

"Let's get a snack. This thing made me dizzy."

"Me too," said Jason.

"I actually thought I was gonna barf while we were on the ride for the fourth time. But now I'm starving. Weird, right?"

"Totally, but I feel the same way. Let's see what we have to eat." Jason got up and then he and Lori hid the headsets under his bed and went down to the kitchen where Jason's mom and his brother were making lunch.

Gregg looked at them strangely. "What are you two *doing* in there?"

Jason quickly replied, "Studying."

"Yeah, right," said Gregg sarcastically. "More like playing video games or something."

Jason hesitated a minute. "No, we're just—"

Lori cut him off, "We looked up some of the mammal stuff we're studying about online and some of the videos were pretty crazy."

"Oh, really? Which ones?" Gregg leaned forward with his elbows on the table, feigning interest.

"That's enough, Gregg," said Debbie.

Jason smiled at Gregg, pleased he was shut down.

"You want a sandwich, Lori?" said Debbie.

"Yeah, that sounds good. I didn't think I was this hungry."

"Oh, that's no problem. Grab a drink and have a seat. I'll make them."

"Thanks, Mrs. Markum."

After lunch, Jason and Lori went back up to Jason's room and shut the door. They were energized and ready.

"I'm a little nervous. I don't know what to expect with this thing," said Jason.

"Yeah, me neither."

"I mean, what if something happens to us?"

Lori stared at Jason, holding up the headsets. "Jason, these are just two headsets. We'll be fine. We're not hopping into a teleporter machine or anything like that. Let's just see what this is all about. Worst case is that it will be disappointing or not work at all. Best case is it will be fun, and we'll get some pics."

Jason kept silent. While he agreed that it was, at the very least, intriguing, "fun" was not the word he would use at this moment.

"All right," Lori began, "Let's use the headsets just like before, only this time I'll insert the Red Chip into the side of mine, and that should do it. The big question now is: where do we go exactly?"

Lori removed the Red Chip from the black box, pried open the side panel on the headset, and snapped the chip into place. She then proceeded to configure the headset with the requested information on the screen. While she was doing this, Jason cleaned up some clothes that were scattered on the floor.

"Look at this," said Lori, pointing to the screen.

Jason leaned in to get a closer look. On the screen was a calendar showing the last full month.

"When was all the drama with Trevor again? Monday?"

"Yeah. In biology."

"Oh, right." Lori shook her head.

Lori was about to click the box in the calendar on the screen for Monday, October 23rd, when there was another knock at Jason's door.

"Yeah?" Jason said through an audible sigh.

"Unlock this. What are you two ... kissing in there or something?" It was Gregg, of course.

Jason rolled his eyes. "Hang on."

Lori quickly grabbed both headsets and placed them back under Jason's bed. She then clicked on an opened webpage that had an article on killer whales, just to complete the façade.

Jason placed his hand on the knob and looked back at Lori who nodded for him to open the door. He opened the door and was immediately attacked by Gregg who tackled him to the ground and started to bend his arm behind his back. He was play fighting, but Jason still hated when he did this.

"Come on wimp, fight back," said Gregg, straddling his brother.

"Get off me, Gregg!"

"You're not studying. You may have Mom fooled, but not me." Gregg then looked at Lori, "And what are *you* looking at?"

Lori leaned in and said just above a whisper, "Not much, dickhead."

Gregg glared at Lori. "What was that?" Gregg then dropped Jason's arm and rose to his feet when Jason's Dad, John, walked by.

"That's enough, Gregg. Leave them alone to study."

"They're not studying," said Gregg, still staring at Lori.

"Yes, we are, jerk," Jason said as he pushed Gregg in the back.

Gregg immediately turned around and pushed him into his dresser causing two picture frames to fall over. John then intervened and forcibly removed Gregg from the room.

"I said enough! Don't start with them again, do you understand me?" yelled John.

Gregg looked down. "Yeah, I understand."

"Now, get out of here and leave them alone."

John watched Gregg leave the room and walk down the hall until he was in his own room. "Sorry, Lori. He knows better."

Lori shook her head, "It's okay, Mr. Markum. My sister can be a pest, too."

John smiled and sighed, "I know. It's what siblings do. Mine did it to me; however, when it comes to interrupting your studying, that I won't have. You two get back to it. He won't bother you anymore."

"Thanks, Mr. Markum."

"You bet." John smiled, backed away, and closed the door.

Jason looked back over at Lori somewhat ashamed and shrugged. "He's such a jerk."

"He is, but so what? Lock the door. No one's gonna bother us for a while now," Lori said with a smile as she reached back under the bed to grab the headsets.

Jason, realizing she was right, turned and locked the door. He then grabbed a spare wooden chair, walked it over to the door, and placed the backrest up underneath the door knob for an extra layer of security.

Jason turned and looked at Lori, "You ready?"

"Let's do this."

Lori resumed setting up, selected Monday, October 23rd on the calendar, and hit Enter. Next, the program asked them to input the time of day they wanted to start with. It also mentioned that they could change the time and date on the screen at any point by clicking the icon on the bottom left part of the screen.

Jason and Lori placed their headsets over their eyes. Both screens inside the headsets now displayed the same countdown clock as before. The countdown got to "1" and both screens went pitch black.

Then it happened.

24.

THE BLACK SCREEN PARTED DOWN THE MIDDLE AND THERE THEY WERE ... in the school janitor's office.

"What the—" said Lori, shrugging her shoulders with her hands upturned toward the ceiling.

"Why are we here? This is weird," said Jason.

"Wait. No, it actually makes some sense. I just remembered I was *in* the janitor's office that morning, bringing Fred something that Shirley in the office asked me to drop off on my way to class."

"Why didn't she just walk it down?"

"Who knows? She seemed rushed and I was in the office because I found a pair of gloves outside that I turned in. Anyway, she gave me these papers ... Dude?"

"What?"

"Forget the fact that we're in Fred's office for a second and realize that *we're in Fred's office on October 23rd!* This might actually be working."

"Are you sure? Why is everything this brownish color," said Jason, waving his arms in front of his face.

"It's called sepia tone. See-pee-yuh. It's like those old timey, black and white photographs that are really more like a reddish-brown color and not so much black and white."

"It's weird you know that. So, everything looks like this?"

"Yep. It was in the user manual. Maybe they'll have color in Phase III. Doesn't matter. Let's start walking to the door and see what's going on. It's seven forty-five, the students should still be outside, and the teachers should either be in their classrooms or on their way there."

"Right."

Jason and Lori opened the office door and walked out into one of the school's empty hallways.

"It's really quiet."

"We don't have sound with these," Lori reminded Jason.

Jason laughed, "No, I mean no one's in the hallway."

Lori nodded. "Let's walk to the left and then follow the hall around to the main office."

"Sounds good. Remember not to stomp your feet."

"Good call."

They quietly marched in place in Jason's room, moving slowly down the hallway of their school, when they came to the main office.

"Stop here," said Lori.

They both stopped and stood still. Jason and Lori looked left and could not believe what they were seeing. They watched Shirley talk to Lori and then hand her an envelope. Lori then turned and walked out of the office right past where Lori and Jason were standing.

They stood silent in Jason's room, stunned at what they just saw.

III.

Surveillance

25.

THE FEW PEOPLE CALLED IN FOR THE EMERGENCY MEETING AT COLLINS Industries were seated around an oval table in the company's executive board room. Everyone there was a little nervous. Through a series of mistakes, oversights, and bad luck, sensitive property had found its way to Southfield's and was now missing.

Ted walked into the conference room, glanced over at the people seated around the table, and headed for his seat at the front. He removed a large coffee, individual milk containers, several sugar packets, and two packs of cupcakes from a brown paper bag. Ted was a first-class stress eater, but no one ever dared mention it to him, especially now.

Ted topped off his coffee, added three sugars, and splashed some milk into his cup and also onto the table. He then stirred his coffee and ripped open the cellophane on both sets of cupcakes. They were all staring at him and then quickly averted their eyes when he looked up. Ted took a bite of one of the cupcakes and, with a mouthful of food, looked up and said, "What do I need to know?"

Everyone shifted in their seats as Jane Stafford sat up in her chair and spoke first.

"Two of our Red Chips are missing. They were in Southfield's when a fire broke out last night. The fire caused an evacuation which led to chaos in the store and—"

Ted put his hand up, cutting Jane off, and said swiftly, "Why were they at Southfield's?"

Jane and Ted had already had this conversation but Ted needed the others in the room to hear it.

"They were sent there by mistake. We needed to send two chips to Akron for further testing and somewhere along the line, the communication to the mailroom jumbled and the Red Chips were sent to Southfield's instead."

"Please tell me you're kidding," said Ted, leaning back in his chair, cleaning his teeth with his tongue.

"I wish I was Ted, although that wouldn't be funny as a joke, either. We're still looking into the breakdown to see how we can prevent this from ever happening again."

"That's great and all, but why weren't the chips reported and returned immediately? Surely Steve knows the sensitivity. He saw them yesterday morning. Right, Steve?" said Ted, looking over at Steve.

Steve was visibly sweating and uncomfortable in his seat.

"I—I made a terrible mistake, Ted, but I need to say one thing," said Steve nervously.

"What's that?"

"There was only one Red Chip, not two. And there was also a user manual." Steve hadn't mentioned the manual to Jane as he had forgotten all about it at the time.

"THE USER MANUAL, TOO?" shouted Ted as he pounded the table with his fist. "Is this a goddamned joke?" Ted's face turned an even darker shade of red. "Why don't we just invite everyone into our research facility with cameras and laptops so they can take notes? Jesus Christ!"

Ted shoved the rest of the cupcake into his mouth and washed it down with some coffee.

Jane spoke up again, "Ted, the package was actually signed for by Pete Davis at Southfield's. He's the young man next to Steve."

Steve looked at Pete and mumbled through another mouthful, "Well, Pete?"

Pete was a bit uncomfortable in this setting, although not really that nervous because he knew that he, technically, didn't do anything wrong. He sat up in his chair and spoke.

"I did open the envelope, which I probably shouldn't have since it wasn't addressed to me, but we get stuff all the time and Steve always tells me to just open whatever it is. Anyway, there was a black box, a user manual with a Roman numeral II on it, and a DVD—"

"What was on the DVD?" said Ted, immediately interrupting Pete.

"The DVD was a five-minute demo loop that we set up for the Collins VR headsets, although we may need another one as I think the sprinklers destroyed our DVD player."

"We'll get you a new one," said Ted.

"Anyway, I saw Steve place both items in the cabinet under our cash register. The technology, if it works, seems awesome, Mr. Collins. I read the manual at lunch," Pete said with a smile.

Roy and Jane returned slight, nervous smiles, hoping to ease the tension a bit. Ted did not smile for many reasons, mostly because he knew Pete did more than simply read the manual. Samantha informed him earlier of that fact. This quick flashback elevated Ted's emotions, and he stood, placed both of his hands flat on the table, leaned forward, and glared at Pete.

"I *know* it's awesome, Pete. That technology is the future of this company. The problem is that those Red Chips were not ready to be sent out to the public yet."

Jane spoke up again. "Ted, there's more."

"What is it?" Ted was still staring at Pete.

"We actually have surveillance footage of Southfield's during the fire alarms. I got it just before this meeting but haven't had a chance to review it. It's loaded in the machine."

Ted turned and looked at Jane. "And what are you waiting for?"

Jane, taking the hint, pointed the remote control at the television which was now displaying the black and white footage from one of the store's ceiling cameras. Despite the water pouring down, the video was fairly clear. They watched about a minute of video where two kids and Pete were, at first, talking and then scrambling to cover up the electronics and hide the headsets under the counter.

"Pause the video. Who the hell are those kids?"

Silence filled the room.

"Pete?" said Ted.

"Yeah?" said Pete, now slumped in his chair.

"Who are those kids?"

"I don't know. Some kids from the high school, I think."

"Do they have names?"

"I'm sure they do."

There was an audible gasp in the room and Steve, through clenched teeth, said, "Honestly, Pete, what are you doing? Give Ted the names."

Ted, steely eyed now, said, "Pete, I'm giving you one last chance to make this right by telling me who they are, otherwise you're fired."

Pete laughed slightly. "You can't fire me. I work for Southfield's, not you."

Ted looked at Steve.

After a moment, Steve caught on and said, "Ted, he's a good kid. A smart-ass, yes, but a good kid. I believe him. I can't fire him."

Ted then turned back to Jane and said, "Jane, can you find out where my son is and send a car to pick him up?"

"Um, of course. Is everything okay?"

"Everything's dandy," said Ted sarcastically through a forced grin. "If these kids are in Parker, then I'm sure my son will know who they are. I want to get to the bottom of this, NOW."

26.

THIRTY MINUTES LATER, TREVOR LEISURELY WALKED INTO THE conference room looking down and typing on his phone. He had on baggy jeans, untied boots, and a hoodie sweatshirt that was unzipped and barely on his shoulders. Ted spoke in a more upbeat tone to hide the real purpose of the meeting from his son. "Everyone, this is my son, Trevor."

Everyone around the table smiled and said hello, except for Pete.

Trevor mumbled something in return and then turned around, looked at his dad, and threw up his arms as if to say, *Why am I here on a Sunday, old man?*

"Come over here and watch this video. It's surveillance footage from Southfield's. You'll see three people in the frame. One of the people is Pete who is sitting right over there," said Ted, pointing at Pete.

Trevor looked over at Pete.

"There are two other kids who Pete thinks are also in the high school. Have a look and let me know if you recognize them."

"What did they do?" said Trevor. He sensed drama and was getting excited.

"Nevermind that. Just have a look."

Ted nodded at Jane who started the video again. Trevor walked a little closer to the screen as the footage played. When the two kids ran away from the scene, Jane paused the video.

Trevor turned and looked at his dad, saying confidently, "Jason Markum and Lori Jenkins."

"Are you sure?" said Ted with a furrowed brow.

"Yep. I caught Jason vandalizing that car last week remember?" Trevor pulled his phone out again.

"It's the same kid?"

"Yeah. I told you he was bad news. He's a lunatic." Trevor then pointed his phone at the screen to take a picture.

"Good eye, son," said Ted, still staring at the screen. Then, noticing Trevor's phone, "Whoa, what are you doing?"

"Taking a picture," said Trevor, focusing the screen on his phone.

Ted grabbed the phone from his son's grip and hit the side button until he heard it click off.

"Hey!" whined Trevor.

"Hey, nothing. No pictures and you're to say nothing to anyone about this. Do you understand me?"

Trevor stared at his father in a way that suggested to Ted that his intimidation was not what it used to be but was still there.

"Fine."

Ted handed the phone back to his son and said, "Thanks, Trevor. This was helpful."

"You rat," snarled Pete, looking directly at Trevor.

"What was that?" said Trevor, taking a step in Pete's direction.

"That's enough. Thank you, son." Ted grabbed his son's shoulders and escorted him in the other direction toward the door. "The car will take you back home. We appreciate your help."

Once Trevor was out the door, Ted closed it, turned around, and said, "Steve?"

"Yes?"

"You and Pete are both fired."

Steve didn't move or say a word.

"Jane?"

"Yes?"

"Contact both sets of parents. I want to meet with them tomorrow. Also, please find a way to get that video onto a phone or something, so I can easily show them what their children are guilty of. I don't want any issues, I just want the Red Chip and the manual back."

"I'll have that in just a few minutes," said Jane, taking out her cell phone and walking out of the room in a hurry.

"Also," said Ted, "Find out if we're missing one or two Red Chips. There seems to be a discrepancy of that fact."

"Will do." Jane left the room and Ted then got up from his chair and walked out behind her.

Steve looked somber and remained slumped in his chair as people began to exit the conference room.

"You know, you just put me in a real bad place, Pete," said Steve, staring at his folded hands.

"Me?" said Pete in a surprised tone.

"All you needed to do was give Ted the two names. No one outside of this room would have ever known it was you."

Pete shook his head and said, "I'm not a rat, Steve. Besides, who's to say he wouldn't have fired us anyway? Why do you want to work for that jerk?"

"Because I have a family to support, that's why. You knew he was going to find those names out somehow. He has the means to get whatever information he wants. I just don't understand how you could be so selfish."

"I'm not trying to be selfish. I'm just not going to be bullied into giving up names. What about you?"

"What?"

"You saw the envelope. You put that stuff in the cabinet. Why didn't *you* pick up the phone and tell Ted immediately?"

Steve knew that Pete had a solid point but there was no reason to keep arguing, especially since they were still in Ted's conference room. They both sat in silence and, after about a minute, Steve got up and walked out of the conference room, leaving Pete alone. Pete then pulled out his phone and sent a text message to Lori.

Hey Lori Trevor just ratted u out. Ted's going to speak with ur parents. Heads up!

27.

JASON AND LORI WERE STILL USING THE VIRTUAL REALITY IN JASON'S room.

"What time is it now?" said Jason, looking around.

"I don't know. For real or here at school?" said Lori.

"At school."

"It's gotta be around 9:00 a.m. since we just walked by ourselves heading to class. Did I just say that?"

"Seriously. This is weird. Can we change the time to right before Mrs. Goldfeather walks back into the classroom? I want to see Trevor snooping through the quizzes."

"Sure, do you remember what time that was?"

"Not really, but try ten-thirty."

"Hang on." Lori raised the headset onto her forehead and leaned closer to the computer. This part was easy. All she needed to do was enter in a new time and *presto!* they would be in a different place that same day.

She typed in 10:30 a.m., hit Enter, and lowered her headset back over her eyes. The countdown clock started its descent from "10." The black screen parted and they were now in the boys' bathroom.

"Ugh. Why are we *here*?" said Lori. This was the last place she wanted to be, even in a virtual world.

"Who knows?" said Jason. "Let's just go and walk quickly back to the classroom. If it's the wrong time, we'll just adjust it again."

As they were heading toward the classroom, they walked right through two students from the class who were presumably on their way to the boys' room.

Mrs. Goldfeather then appeared in the doorway, and they both stopped on instinct, even though she could not see them.

"This is it. Let's go. Trevor is going to walk up to the desk any second. How do we capture the image?" said Jason.

"It's on my headset. I just need to push a button that's over my right ear."

"I didn't even realize it was there." Jason was now feeling around the right side of his headset.

"It's hard to see. I wouldn't have noticed it if I didn't read it in the manual. But only I can do it since I'm connected directly to the laptop."

They proceeded into the classroom and stood right next to Mrs. Goldfeather's desk. Moments later, Trevor walked up to the desk and started looking at the first few quizzes that were on top of a larger pile of papers.

"Take the picture!" said Jason anxiously.

"I am. I've taken like five already."

"Any chance you can take video?"

"Not with this."

Lori snapped off several more pictures that clearly showed Trevor rifling through the students' quizzes.

Jason then let out a sigh. "Let's take a break. I don't need to relive the moment of getting yelled at again."

"Sounds good to me."

Jason and Lori removed their headsets and were, once again, a little dizzy. But this time wasn't as bad as when they rode The Night Train earlier.

"Want something to drink?" asked Jason.

"Yeah. My mouth is totally dry."

"Mine too. I'll be right back. See if you got those photos."

"Will do."

Lori sat back down at the desk and started typing on the laptop while Jason unbarricaded the door and went to find some drinks for them in the kitchen. The screen on the laptop asked Lori if she wanted the fifteen photos that she took sent to her phone or somewhere else. Lori clicked on "somewhere else," and the screen prompted her to either enter a cell phone number or an email address. She entered her email address and, moments later, was alerted that she had new messages.

Lori clicked on her email icon and, incredibly, there they were—fifteen new emails. She clicked on the first message and then double-clicked the attachment. After a few seconds, she shook her head in disbelief. Just like they both witnessed, Trevor was at Mrs. Goldfeather's desk looking at the first quiz from last Monday.

Jason returned with two bottles of water. "Any luck?"

Lori swiveled around in the desk chair, pointed at the screen, and smiled.

Jason leaned in and his face lit up with excitement when he saw the pictures.

"Well, I'm totally off the hook for *that* one. We need to go back so we can see him letting the air out of Mrs. Goldfeather's tires at lunch."

"That's next."

"Let's finish these waters and then hop back—"

There was yet another knock at the door, this time from Jason's dad.

"Hey, Jason?"

"Yeah Dad?"

"Got a sec?"

Lori put the headsets under the desk but did not unplug them. She then grabbed her textbook and notebook from under the bed and hid the wires underneath. She was tired of snooping around and would just come up with a story if one of Jason's family members got on her about the headsets.

Jason opened the door.

"How's it going in here?" said John, looking around.

"Not too bad. We're getting a lot done," answered Jason, cool as a cucumber. He couldn't believe this was working.

"That's great. Sorry to bother you but I wanted to let you know that you two are on your own for dinner. Mom and I are going out again. Also, Ted Collins, Trevor's father, just called a meeting for tomorrow night with you guys, your mom, myself, and Lori's mom. His secretary said it was urgent but didn't say what it was about. Pretty strange, right? You guys have any idea since you're in class with his son?"

Almost in unison, they both shook their heads.

"Does this have to do with what went on last Monday?" said John.

Jason, sensing that Mr. Collins did not mention the headsets said, "Could be. Maybe Mr. Hagen finally realized that I didn't do anything wrong."

"Well, Mr. Hagen will be there, too, I was told. Anyway, we'll discuss that later. You two get back to it and here," John took a twenty-dollar bill out of his wallet and threw it on Jason's bed, "Get some pizza, or whatever you want, on me."

"Thanks, Mr. Markum," said Lori.

"Yeah, thanks Dad."

John smiled, left the room, and closed the door.

Jason waited a second and then turned to Lori. "We need a plan." Then, seeing Lori's expression change as she read something on her phone, said, "What is it?"

Lori held up the text message she just read from Pete so that Jason could see it. Jason leaned forward on his bed and read Lori's screen.

"This is not good. I was hoping the meeting wasn't about the headsets after all, but it definitely is. What do we do?" Jason started to panic.

"We need to log back in and finish getting the evidence. That's what."

"Then what?" Jason winced in pain.

"You okay?"

"Not really. My stomach hurts all of a sudden."

"It's nerves. Don't worry about it. Just remember, you got in trouble for something that you didn't do and now we're getting you out of it."

"I know, but we also stole this equipment."

"I *borrowed* it, remember?" Lori said with a smile. "Listen, let's get all the evidence and then, at the meeting, I'll admit to taking the equipment for a specific purpose. More importantly, we'll get you off the hook."

"Seems risky."

"It's not. We'll be telling the truth and exposing Trevor for who he is—a total liar."

Jason thought for a moment, looked down, and then back up at Lori. "We did this together."

"No, it's—"

Jason held up his hand and shook his head. "I'm not letting you take the blame. That's insane. For now, though, you're right, let's just finish what we started."

"To be continued," said Lori, smirking. She chugged the rest of her water and threw the bottle near the trash can. She handed Jason his headset and began to punch more keys on the keyboard.

"Teacher's parking lot around 12:10 p.m.?"

"Yeah." Jason placed his headset on the desk and secured the wooden chair back underneath the door knob.

28.

"HER NAME IS LORI JENKINS," SAID ONE OF THE VALHALLA EMPLOYEES seated at the main computer. Samantha and Nicholas Foster, Samantha's boss (and also one of the several people hidden behind the glass at the July meeting with Ted), stood behind her looking up at the main screen on the wall. The wall showed Lori's school I.D. photo along with all of her personal information, including her address and phone number.

Without taking his eyes off the screen, Nicholas took a sip of his break-room coffee. "How the hell did she get access, Samantha? I thought it was only the one high school kid, Pete."

Samantha was stunned like the rest of the group but, knowing that she needed to maintain her composure, looked right at Nicholas. "We are trying to understand that as well." She then tried to smooth this over. "I was told by Ted that there was one missing Red Chip, but this Pete kid did not have a chance to access the program. He merely entered in his information and was then cut off. Somehow this same chip wound up in the hands of Lori Jenkins."

"How far did she get in the program?"

Samantha hesitated too much this time and weakly replied, "All the way."

"All the w—"

"She accessed the Look-Back and went back about a week. It looks like it was for some issue at school as best we could tell. Nothing serious."

Nicholas looked at the wall and then back at Samantha. "It's *very* serious, Samantha. Not only was no one supposed to have access to this other than Ted, who knows he's being watched like a hawk, but now two kids have accessed it and know about it. And the fact that they accessed it is only part of the problem."

Samantha knew Nicolas well enough to know that she had to prompt him to finish his thought. It was one of his more annoying qualities. "What's the other part?"

"Who *else* now knows?" Nicholas paused for a moment before continuing. "Do you really think that the two of them have kept this a secret? They must have told *somebody*. It's not an overstatement to think that this whole project which, as you know, has us currently working on enhancements to expand the range of these chips, could be compromised if enough people simply hear about this, much less experience it. The rumors they create, even if exaggerated, could very well still be accurate."

"I think that's assuming a lot. We haven't even spoken to this Lori Jenkins yet to understand her motivations nor can we link her to Pete despite all signs pointing to—"

"There's more," said the woman at the computer, interrupting Samantha.

"I'm sorry?" said Samantha.

"When Lori accessed the system, there were two headsets plugged in. There may have been someone else with her."

Silence filled the space as Samantha started twisting the ring she wore on her right index finger.

"Can we tell who the other person is?" asked Samantha. This was going from bad to worse, and her explanations to Nicholas were losing credibility.

"We think we can. The system was accessed on Lori's laptop, but she was not at her house when she logged in."

"Jesus," said Nicholas, turning away from the screen.

"Hang on," said Samantha, putting up her hand. "Where was she?"

"We have an IP address that matches another home in Oak Brook. Could be a friend."

"Last name?"

"Working on that and the street address now, but I'll need a couple of hours."

Samantha closed her eyes and stood perfectly still. She typically did this when she received a slew of new information and needed to process it quickly. Some found it a little strange, but no one ever questioned her as she could make up contingency plans on the spot.

"Okay, find the address and anything else you can about who the person is with Lori. In the meantime, I'm calling Ted. We spoke before about him smashing all remaining Red Chips. It's clear that at least one hasn't been smashed and may not even be in his possession."

"Samantha, how are you going to get it back if he doesn't even have it?" inquired Nicholas. Despite being the one in charge, he was now starting to feel the heat. After all, he's the one who must answer to the powers that be.

"One step at a time. There will be a plan after I speak with Ted. Excuse me."

Samantha left the main room and proceeded down the hall into her office, slamming the door. She walked over to her desk, placed both of her hands flat on the surface, leaned back, hung her head, and breathed deeply for a few minutes. She then sat down at her desk and dialed Ted's number.

Ted had a small spring in his step as he walked into his house. His son had identified Jason and Lori in the surveillance video about two hours earlier, which was an enormous relief to him.

His phone rang in his pocket and, as he pulled it out, he stopped walking. His heart sank a little because he knew it was *them*. He couldn't ignore the call. He didn't want them showing up at the office in front of his employees, or worse, his home. They still had no idea of the magnitude of this whole saga and, as far as Ted was concerned, it would stay that way. He hit the green button and sat down on the couch in his home office.

"Yeah?" answered Ted.

"Ted, we've had a change in plans since our meeting in your office. You are not to destroy any Red Chips, but hand them over to us fully intact."

Ted grinned. "What's the matter, Samantha? You don't trust me?"

Samantha rolled her eyes and said, "I think you already know the answer to that. By the way, is there anything else you'd like to share about this, Ted?"

Ted shifted in his seat and had a three-second debate in his head about whether he should tell Samantha about Jason and Lori or just play dumb.

"Like what?"

"Like, I don't know, other features that you forgot to mention when you were here ... or at any other point along the development timeline."

Samantha was also notified that day that there was a possibility that the chip already had a built-in enhancement that allowed a user to widen the search radius when exploring in the Look-Back. It would help the engineers out tremendously if Ted confirmed this and provided instructions on how to access this feature. Samantha knew her team would figure it out eventually but since she had him in the palm of her hand, it was time to get more out of him.

"Samantha, I really don't know what you're talking abou—"

"How's the family, Ted?" said Samantha, smiling, her feet now up on her desk. She had absolutely no patience for his crap right now.

Ted wiped the top of his now perspiring bald head and then wiped his hand on his pant leg. He shifted in his seat and was struggling for what to say next. He had a hard time believing that Samantha would really harm his family especially since she never gave any indication of having those thoughts or behaviors during their correspondence over the previous two and a half years. He figured the pressure must be coming from someone else; someone higher up.

After what seemed like several minutes, but was only about fifteen seconds, Ted relented and said in a muted tone, "I assume you're referring to the search radius?"

Samantha dropped her feet off her desk and sat upright in her chair. She clicked her pen and grabbed a blank piece of paper that was sitting on her desk. "Now we're getting somewhere, Ted. Good boy. I'm listening."

Ted took a deep breath. "The range can go up to a hundred miles from wherever the phone was during the period, but you need to understand that the quality of the video is not as sharp the farther out you go and we don't know why. That's the truth, Samantha."

"I see. And how do we access it?"

"I don't know the specifics off-hand. Look, I'm getting everything back tomorrow. I can get the chip to you, along with detailed instructions, on Tuesday. That is an absolute promise."

"And how certain are you that you're getting the chip back?"

"I believe they have the chip. I mean, I *know* they have it. I just need to get it from them in a non-confrontational way. I've set up a meeting with them and their parents for tomorrow night." Ted could not catch himself in time and knew that he just said too much.

"Who's *they*, Ted?" Samantha knew she had him now. Ted could not find the words so she continued. "More kids used the Red Chip, didn't they?"

Another pause. "I can't confirm that, but I guess it's possible," Ted lied.

"So that makes three teenagers who know about this and I believe you just mentioned parents, which makes how many, Ted?"

"I ... I'm not sure."

"Well, if it's six parents, then that makes it a total of nine. The math isn't too hard, Ted. This is a real issue. How much longer until over twenty people are aware of this? A hundred? Your carelessness may prove to be fatal. I hope you can live with that burden."

"Now, hang on a second," Ted barked, finding his voice. He moved to the edge of the couch. "Let's not overreact Samantha. These are kids for Chrissakes! They aren't spies from some foreign country. For all they know, it's a goddamn video game and nothing more."

"For your sake, I hope you're right; however, I'm not a big fan of hope so once we have the Red Chip back here, we'll be sure to really understand what they know and whether they believe it was just a video game."

"Be reasonable, Samantha. Do you want me to say something when I meet with them tomorrow?"

"Say nothing, Ted. You've done enough. Just get us what we need and we'll deal with Lori and her friend at the right time."

Ted's eyes went wide, and he said, "How did you know?" But then quickly realized that these people have their methods of watching.

"I'll tell you what. If you'd like to help your cause, tell me Lori's friend's name. We're having a little trouble with that."

This, of course, was another lie, as they would eventually uncover the house using GPS coordinates.

"Promise me you won't hurt these kids, Samantha."

"I cannot say with certain—"

"PROMISE ME!" Ted thundered.

Samantha hesitated and put her feet back on her desk, silently admiring her puppet master skills.

"I promise we won't hurt anyone." Samantha paused for another moment and wiped some crumbs off of her desk. "Now, what's the friend's name?"

The name was on the tip of Ted's tongue but, either from a lack of common sense or an abundance of nerve, he now wanted more.

"What's the technology going to be used for?"

"You know I can't get into that, Ted."

Ted laid back on his couch and placed his free hand behind his head. "Well, you see, it's funny, Samantha. I'm all of a sudden having trouble remembering names." When she didn't reply, Ted pressed on, "With a little help, I think I'll also remember how to access the search radius."

Silence filled the air until Samantha broke it. "All right, Ted. You're in deep enough, I see no reason why you can't be made aware of one of the uses." She took a breath and continued, "This technology will give us the upper hand with many adversaries and even allies overseas. Not to mention some political people right here in the United States."

"Upper hand?"

"Yes. You see many officials in the government, some you've heard of and some you haven't, always want short-cuts to cutting deals on all sorts of initiatives around the world. Behind the curtain of the lies they spew to TV cameras and microphones, it's really a dirty business. This technology will allow us to potentially expose cover-ups, obtain critical information, and convince certain players into seeing many things our way. Essentially—"

"Blackmail," finished Ted.

"That's an offensive word, but it sounds like you've picked this up pretty quickly. Not bad, Ted."

More silence filled the air until Samantha broke it again. "You still there?"

Ted stared at the carpet between his feet, his elbow resting on his knee. "I—I honestly can't believe this. We've built something awful."

Samantha rolled her eyes again. "Don't be naïve, Ted. If you didn't build it, we would have found someone else. Honestly, did you think you were building a video game for the United States Government? These backroom deals go on all the time. Too many people talk about it as far as I'm concerned but it's safe to assume that most Americans have no idea what's going on with our so-called diplomats. It's a game of chicken every single day, and now we have an advantage over everyone. At least until others get their hands on this, or similar, technology.

"Now, back to our original discussion. Hopefully this new information has jogged your memory. What's the name of Lori's friend?"

Ted sighed and then said softly, "Jason."

"Good. Jason what?"

Another pause, and then, "Markum. M-A-R-K-U-M."

"Thank you, Ted. One last thing."

"What's that?"

"Where's the meeting tomorrow?" "I've asked for it here. Why?"

"What time?"

"Around 6 p.m. I don't want you people here again, Samantha."

"Relax. After the meeting, you will meet a representative of ours at a location yet to be determined. I'll text you beforehand. She will approach you casually, but you are to turn over the Red Chip immediately and not discuss it. She will be wearing a pin of a house sparrow on her shirt collar, so you'll know she's your contact."

"I don't want her or anyone else trying anything, especially in front of my son."

"These are trained professionals, Mr. Collins. She won't if you simply do what I'm telling you to do. Got it?"

"Yes. Anything else?"

"Yes. Don't forget to include the instructions that we just discussed. Enjoy the rest of your Sunday."

Samantha ended the call with a smile on her face. Ted remained on his couch wiping more sweat off his forehead. He had clearly met his match with Samantha and, only now, started to regret his decision to move ahead with the Phase II technology.

29.

Monday

THE NEXT DAY AT SCHOOL, JASON AND LORI MET UP DURING THE MORNING biology class break. Both were totally exhausted, especially Lori.

"I didn't sleep too well. How about you?" asked Jason.

"I think I slept three hours. I'm totally shot," said Lori.

Trevor then walked over, grinning from ear to ear and rubbing his hands together.

"Well, well, well. If it isn't the two thieves. You two ready for the big meeting later today? I heard the police might even be there. It should be exciting. My dad asked me to come, too. It'll be fun to watch you two try to explain your way out of this."

"We didn't steal anything," said Jason.

"Oh, you don't have to explain it to me," said Trevor as he laughed and held up his hands. "Trust me, it wasn't that hard to see you two on camera. The surveillance footage is clear as day."

Jason forgot about the surveillance footage at Southfield's. His stomach started acting up but he managed to mutter, "So is what we have."

Lori elbowed Jason's arm.

"What was that, thief?"

"Nothing. You'll see," said Jason.

"Yeah, right. I'm sure it's nothing. My dad's telling me you two losers might be suspended when all of this is over. How embarrassing. No one will ever forget *that*, and you'll have to go through high school with that reputation. Sucks to be you two."

Lori spoke up. "Trevor, just get lost. We'll settle this later at the meeting."

Trevor laughed again and walked away. "Yes, we will. Yes, we will. Don't forget, it starts at six in my dad's office."

"We know, thanks," said Lori, rolling her eyes. She then turned to Jason. "Sorry, I didn't mean to hit you. I just don't want him to see this coming at all. I'm going to the Office Center after school to print out the photos and make a few stops."

"Okay. What stops?"

Mrs. Goldfeather got up from her desk and walked to the center of the classroom.

"All right everyone. Take your seats."

"We'll talk later," said Lori as she walked back to her desk.

Immediately after school, Lori took her bike to the Office Center to print out the photos she downloaded the day and night before. She copied and pasted all of the photos into a document so she could print multiple copies of one file instead of printing each picture individually. It was also cheaper to do it this way since the store charges per page.

After printing the photos, Lori headed back to the school to speak with Mr. Hagen before the meeting. Up until that moment, she wasn't sure if she was going to take it upon herself to speak with him beforehand. She knew it wasn't really her place to do so, but she also wanted Mr. Hagen to digest this crazy information beforehand.

As Lori neared the school, she came to the corner where the deli, always overflowing with students both in the morning and right after school, was located. A woman, who seemed lost, was looking back between her phone and the street signs. The woman caught Lori's eye and approached her with a friendly smile across her face.

"Excuse me, but can you tell me where the town library is? I think my phone is acting up and my GPS isn't working," said the woman, showing her phone's screen to Lori.

Lori found the question a little strange but didn't really give it much thought. "Oh, sure, it's actually right up this street." Lori pointed to where she came from. "It's on the right, behind the fire station. You'll see a sign that says Municipal Plaza."

"Municipal Plaza. Great. Thank you so much."

"I like your pin," complimented Lori.

The woman looked down, touching the pin in the shape of a bird on her collar. "Oh, thank you. It was a gift from my nephew. You have a good day."

"You too."

Lori then rode around to the front of the school while the woman walked on and dialed her phone. "It's me. Did you get it? She looked right at the screen."

The voice on the other end said, "Yes, confirmed. We'll keep you updated for the location of the handoff later on. Good work."

Mr. Hagen was reluctant to meet with Lori but agreed to give her five minutes, which quickly turned into fifteen. He was stunned at what he saw in the photos, and even more stunned at how she got the pictures, but not surprised that Trevor was the cause of this whole situation. Lori informed him that she was going to share the same printouts with Jason's parents and her mom prior to the meeting, but that Trevor and Mr. Collins wouldn't know about these until the meeting. His reaction was expressionless but that was only until Lori walked out of his office. He closed the door and called his wife. He had never been so excited to have a late-night meeting with three sets of angry parents before in his life.

30.

LORI ARRIVED AT JASON'S HOUSE AT 4:30 P.M. AFTER GETTING A TEXT from her mom to meet her there. Lori's mom was horrified to learn the real reason for the meeting from Jason a few minutes earlier, but she wasn't going to make a scene in front of the Markums. They'd been a great support to her over the last two years, and she would be respectful to them in their home.

Jason sat on the living room couch with both of his parents and Lori's mom, Paula.

"Lori, come in here and sit down," said Paula abruptly.

"Hi, Mr. Markum, Mrs. Markum," said Lori plopping down on the open seat on the couch.

"Hi, Lori," said John. "Jason was just telling us that you both took headsets from Southfield's on Saturday night. Is this true?"

Lori looked at Jason who looked back at her and nodded. She then looked at her mom and said, "Yes."

"Is that what this meeting is about with Ted Collins?" asked Paula.

"Most likely, yes."

John then spoke up, "You two realize that this man is not the friendliest person in the world, and we wouldn't put it past him to possibly get you both suspended, or even worse."

"That's not gonna happen, Mr. Markum."

"Lori!" interrupted Paula.

"I'm sorry?" said John.

Lori sat up and moved to the edge of her seat. "I need to show you all something, and all I ask is that you let me explain the whole thing. It's going to sound crazy, but I can prove what I'm about to tell you."

"Lori, we don't have time for stories. We're talking about a serious crime." Paula was trying to remain as calm as possible, but it was getting hard.

"I know, but I did it for a reason."

"*We* did it for a reason," said Jason.

"Sorry?" said Paula.

"It was both of us, Mrs. Jenkins."

"I understand, but there's still no good reason to do something like this."

"Just give her a chance. Trust me, you need to hear this. You all do." Jason looked at his parents.

"All right," Paula replied with a sigh. "I don't see how this is going to help but go ahead."

"Go ahead, Lori," said John.

For the next several minutes, Lori and Jason explained the new Look-Back technology and how they were using it the day before up in Jason's room.

"This is absurd. Lori, enough of this nonsense," Paula said after they were done speaking.

"I thought you two were studying," added Debbie disappointingly.

Lori proceeded to unzip her bag and pull out a file folder containing multiple copies of the pages she had printed. She handed them all out, and Jason couldn't help but smile a little bit.

"What's this?" asked John.

"Take a look. What you see are the exact images of what we saw yesterday using the headsets and, more importantly, what *actually* occurred at school. As you can see, Jason did nothing wrong."

John flipped through the pages of photos, "I don't understand—you took these pictures at school? Didn't anyone see you taking them?"

"No. We took them yesterday while using the headsets. This is the Look-Back feature we just told you about. We stood right next to Trevor when he was looking at everyone's quizzes and then later when he was letting the air out of Mrs. Goldfeather's tires," said Jason.

"I'm sorry, but I don't see how this will hold up as being credible."

"Honestly, who's going to believe this?" backed up Debbie.

"Mr. Collins will. *He* knows it's real," said Jason. "This technology does not exist anywhere else. All Mr. Collins wants is the chip back before the technology gets out and his competitors can copy it. At least, that's my guess."

"First of all, I'm not so sure it's that simple, and secondly, how do you know that?" said John.

"I was texting Pete last night. He was in the meeting when Trevor ratted us out," said Lori.

"Who the hell is Pete?" said Debbie. Debbie rarely used that kind of language, but this was just too confusing.

"Pete works at Southfield's. He a senior at Parker. He's a really nice guy. He was also fired by Ted during the meeting."

"WHAT MEETING?" shouted Paula holding her hands up to the sides of her face, her patience finally lost. "I'm sorry. This is all ... a little too much. Can someone please tell me what meeting you're all talking about?"

Lori spoke up in an even tone, "There was a meeting yesterday at Collins Industries about these missing headsets."

Jason interrupted, "But, it's not the headsets he's worried about, Mrs. Jenkins," said Jason, trying his best to diffuse the situation. "It's the Red Chip that we mentioned. That's what's needed for the Look-Back."

"And this Red Chip, or whatever, is what you used to take these pictures?"

"Exactly."

"Okay, so what happened at this meeting yesterday?" asked Debbie.

"Right, and also, just out of curiosity, why was this guy fired if he didn't do anything?" said John.

"Because he didn't identify us on the store's surveillance footage."

"*Surveillance* footage? I can't even." Paula was now on the brink of a full-scale meltdown.

"Mom, it's okay. It's just the security cameras that hang from the ceiling at Southfield's. We're not denying anything."

"That really doesn't make me feel any better, Lori," said Paula, shaking her head.

Lori then leaned back on the couch and looked down.

"Hold on a second," said John, now moving toward the edge of the couch and sitting up straighter. "Pete works for Southfield's, right?"

"Up until yesterday, yeah," said Jason.

"And he was fired by someone who he doesn't work for because he wouldn't identify you guys to him?"

"That's right," said Lori.

"That's ridiculous."

"I know! And Pete's boss, Steve, was also fired, and he doesn't work for Mr. Collins either."

"I'm lost," said Paula, throwing up her arms.

"John, who cares about the guys who were fired? Can we stay focused on our children here?" said Debbie, visibly annoyed.

"We are, Deb," said John. "I'm just trying to get a handle on this whole situation. That's all."

They all sat in silence for a few moments when Debbie spoke again, in a softer tone. "So, what are we going to do?"

John gathered his thoughts and then stood and walked behind the couch. He started to pace the room, looking down at the ground with one hand on the side of his face. "We are dealing with a situation that has gone completely off the rails.

If these images are true, then Jason clearly did nothing wrong but has been blamed not only by Trevor but by the school principal as well! Let's not forget that point. Given Ted's influence in Oak Brook, that likely won't change unless we show him and the others exactly what went on last Monday. I almost hate to say it because they still broke the law, but Jason and Lori are absolutely right."

"Ted won't listen," said Debbie, dismissing her husband's remarks.

"Actually, he *will* listen because that's going to be the condition of him getting his Red Chip back. Ted couldn't care less about a broken law or two," said John.

"That whole family is awful," offered Paula.

John nodded in agreement. "That is becoming more apparent, Paula. And because of that, there's not going to be any reasoning with this man. So, here's what we're gonna do." John then turned toward Lori. "Lori, where are the headsets and the Red Chip now?"

"At our house," said Lori.

"Good. You and your mom head home, pack them up and just relax for a bit. Keep those printouts safe. I'm calling Ted and Roger and we're having the meeting at school, not at Collins Industries. Ted's not running this meeting. I'm going to tell him that we have his property and will turn it back over to him. No doubt he will agree to drop everything."

"And give Pete and his boss their jobs back," said Jason.

"Yeah," said Lori, her eyes lighting up.

"Why not?" said John, shrugging with a smile. "You're right. They shouldn't have lost their jobs."

"What about Trevor?" Lori asked.

"We'll save that for the meeting, but it's going to be up to Mr. Hagen and Ted how they want to deal with Trevor."

"Do you really think this will work, John?" said Paula, feeling slightly more optimistic.

"I honestly have no idea, but it's our only real option of getting this guy off our backs and putting this nonsense to bed before it really gets out of hand."

"Mr. Markum?" said Lori.

"Yeah?"

"Thanks."

"Don't thank me yet, Lori. We're not quite done."

Lori and Paula left Jason's house and headed home. Debbie made some pasta for the three of them to eat quickly so they weren't starving at the meeting. The last thing they needed was to be devoid of energy with grumbling stomachs. She was still uneasy about why her son got mixed up in something like this, but there was also a small part of her that was proud of him for standing up for himself and taking a risk. For now, though, she was going to keep that praise to herself.

The phone call to Ted was surprisingly easy. Once Ted heard that the headsets, and more importantly, the Red Chip were safe, he agreed to meet at the school. John did not go into the other details but did mention that there was more to the story than just petty theft. Roger Hagen agreed as well and was a little surprised to hear that Ted didn't put up a fight about the venue change.

31

THE SCHOOL WAS TOTALLY DIFFERENT AT NIGHT. THE PARKING LOT WAS empty except for two cars. The lights were off and no one was running around. There was no crossing guard. Nothing except silence.

Jason's dad parked the car in the teacher's lot and he, Debbie, and Jason got out and headed up the stairs toward the main entrance. The door was locked, not unusual for this time of day, so they rang the intercom. After a moment, Mr. Hagen appeared and let them in. He then unlocked the door so he wouldn't need to get up again for the others. Pleasantries were exchanged and they walked into his office where more small talk was made. Jason thought his office was going to be a little cramped for all the people, but then again, Mr. Hagen did seem nervous and Jason wouldn't be surprised if he chose his office to intentionally keep this meeting uncomfortable and therefore brief. And that was just fine with him.

A few minutes later Lori and Paula showed up and were seated.

Ted and Trevor left their house just as Lori, Jason, and the others arrived at school. While Ted didn't say anything out loud to his son, he would make sure they intentionally arrived at the school a few minutes late since he was strong-armed into changing the meeting's location at the last minute. He could be spiteful that way.

As he and his son came to a stoplight in the middle of Oak Brook, a black SUV pulled up alongside Ted's car. Ted looked over as the heavily tinted window of the passenger door slowly rolled down revealing a face with sunglasses. Ted's eyes drifted up and he froze. While he didn't recognize that particular face as one of the goons he had already met, it didn't matter. Mr. Sunglasses at Night Man knew exactly who Ted was and as the light turned green and the SUV turned left and sped away, Ted felt a wave of nervousness wash over him. He wondered where these people kept coming from. Are they tracking his car? Watching his house? Maybe he really was over his head with these people. How was he ever going to sell these Red Chips to the public when they're hounding him over *one* missing chip? Ted's mind continued racing and he became so lost in thought that he didn't even see the next traffic light turn red.

"Dad! Red light!" shouted Trevor.

"Wha—" muttered Ted as he snapped back into the present moment. He then leaned back in his seat, straightened his arms, and slammed down on the brake pedal. He instinctively reached his right arm to catch Trevor even though they both had their seatbelts on. The car came to a stop only a few feet over the white line. Thankfully, no one was in the crosswalk. While they most likely would not have been hit, they would have definitely been startled.

"Are you okay?" asked Trevor.

Ted regrouped. "I'm fine. Sorry. My mind was somewhere else."

Finally, at 6:45 p.m., headlights reflected onto the ceiling of Mr. Hagen's office. As all those present turned around to peer out onto the front of the school, they saw Ted and Trevor get out of a fancy sports car that was parked in the fire lane.

"Typical," muttered John under his breath, shaking his head.

The office got very quiet when both Ted and his son appeared. They both shook hands with Mr. Hagen and sat down. John got up to shake hands with Ted but noticed that a return handshake was not going to happen, so he sat back down.

Mr. Hagen spoke. "First, I want to thank all of you for being here tonight. I'm sure that we can come to an understanding of what happened and learn how to move for—"

"Your kids stole my property!" declared Ted startling almost everyone in the room.

This was Ted's strategy—appear agitated to control the meeting even though drawing too much attention to this whole thing wasn't in his best interest.

"Ted, please," said Mr. Hagen.

"Please nothing. These kids should be suspended. Remember our discussion earlier?"

"Ted." Roger's elbows were on the desk as he motioned with his hands to try and keep the meeting civilized.

"What discussion?" asked John.

"We met yesterday as I couldn't get a hold of Ted during the week," said Roger.

"Why were we not included?" said Debbie.

"It's—" began Mr. Hagen.

Ted held up his hand cutting off Roger Hagen, pulled out his phone, tapped it a few times and handed it to Debbie. "It doesn't matter. Just watch your kids carefully."

"What is this?"

"It's surveillance video from Southfield's the night of the fire. Notice anyone familiar?" mocked Ted.

Debbie, Paula, and John watched the surveillance footage of Jason and Lori throwing the tarp over the register followed by Lori ducking under the cover and then coming back out with a shopping bag.

"We know they took your headsets. Why are you showing us this?" said John.

"It's proof."

"Ted. They've already admitted it. That's why we're here. That's all the proof you need," said John, raising his voice slightly.

"Okay. So where are the police?" said Ted, glaring at Roger and also not really wanting the police anywhere near this situation.

"Not so fast, Ted," said Roger.

"Excuse me?"

"There is a larger issue here and it goes back to why Lori and Jason claim they took the headsets in the first place."

"Well, I'm all ears."

Trevor began to fidget in his seat.

"Lori stopped by after school today to speak with me. I would like her to tell the story."

Everyone looked at Lori who sheepishly said, "I think Jason should tell it."

"Okay," said Ted, rolling his eyes and then looking at his phone. "Can *someone* please tell this story, before I call the police myself?"

"Put your phone away, Ted," warned Debbie.

"Why should I?"

"Because we're all here to make this right," said John. "Let Jason say his piece. Trust me, you're going to want to hear this."

"Fine." Ted placed his phone in his inside jacket pocket.

"Go ahead, Jason," said Roger.

Jason sat up in his chair. "Okay. Last Monday, Trevor was the one who looked at everyone's quizzes in Mrs. Goldfeather's class and then let the air out of her tires later at lunch."

"You're such a liar. Nice try, Jason," snarled Trevor, sitting up in his seat.

"Quiet," said Ted to his son. He then looked back at Jason. "That's a large accusation you're making, especially considering my son and the safety patrol officer saw you with the gizmo to let the air out of her tires. I believe you were caught red-handed in both instances, Jason."

Jason looked over at Lori and nodded.

Lori then leaned down and opened the Southfield's shopping bag.

"What else did you take?"

"Ted, please be quiet for a second and let them finish," said Paula, finding her own voice in the tense room.

Ted stopped talking.

Lori handed out the printed copies to Ted and Trevor.

"What's this?"

"Yeah, what is this?" echoed Trevor.

"I said quiet, Trevor."

"Look carefully, Trevor, and you tell us," smirked Lori.

Jason noticed a small smile form on Mr. Hagen's face that quickly disappeared when Ted lifted his head to speak.

"Why don't they have copies too?" asked Ted.

"They've seen these already," said Lori.

"Yeah, well, what does this prove?" said Ted, rattling the papers in front of his face.

"Ask your son," said John.

Ted sighed at John and then looked at his son. "Trevor, what am I looking at here?"

"This is such crap, Lori." Trevor stood, prompting Ted to stand and stare down at his son until Trevor sat back down in his chair.

Jason then broke the silence. "Mr. Collins. Your technology works. These images were taken using the headsets. The first images are of Trevor searching through the quizzes, then of me confronting him, followed by Mrs. Goldfeather walking in to see us both at her desk. The next set is your son letting the air out of her tires with the tire gauge and then placing it in my pocket when the safety patrol officer was not looking."

The office was completely silent as Ted sat still looking at the images. "Well, you obviously did not do these things, Jason, but you still stole the equipment and you need to be held accountable for it."

"With all due respect, Ted," said John, "Your son not only committed the incidents, but then lied about them. Anything on him?"

"There are two separate things here, John. What my son did is minor and will be dealt with at home. What your kid did is illegal."

Roger interjected, "Let's take a breath for a moment. May I propose a compromise?"

"Fine with me," said Paula, hoping to be done with this already.

"It depends what it is. Actually, you know what? We're not going any further with this until I see everything," said Ted.

"Fair enough," said Roger. He then looked at Lori and nodded.

Lori's mom handed the shopping bag over to Ted who looked inside. He removed the black box, opened it, and felt relieved to see the Red Chip. He closed the box and placed it inside his sports jacket's pocket.

"Good," he said. "Roger, on second thought, forget the compromise. My son will apologize to Mrs. Goldfeather in the morning and I'm pressing charges on these two. I will not have my own property used against me. I'll remind you again of our little discussion from earlier."

"What is this, Ted?" said John.

"This is business, John."

"Business?"

Debbie interjected, "Your money doesn't give you the right to call the shots on who gets in trouble and who doesn't."

"It does, actually," said Ted, grinning slyly.

Trevor offered the same grin to Jason and Lori.

"Not tonight, it doesn't," said Mr. Hagen.

Ted laughed. "Since this is probably your first and last year at this school, Roger, I'd be really careful."

Roger stood from his desk and opened the door that led into the waiting area.

"Jason, Lori, and Trevor. I'd like you to leave the room for a few moments, so I can speak with your parents in private."

All three looked at their parents and then quietly got up and headed out into the main part of the office.

Mr. Hagen closed his office door, sat back down, and pulled out his phone. He tapped it a few times and then turned up the volume. What everyone in his office was now listening to was the coffee shop conversation where Ted threatened Roger's job if he didn't leave his son alone and suspend Jason instead.

"So, you recorded our private conversation? Good for you."

"You're repulsive," said Paula, looking squarely at Ted.

Mr. Hagen put both of his hands up and raised his voice. "Ladies and Gentlemen, here's what's going to happen. There will be no informing the police of anything. Ted, you have your property back and these kids admitted to stealing it. They did it to prove Jason's innocence. Lori didn't have to get involved at all, but she stuck her neck out for her friend, which is extremely admirable, by the way. If you decide to press charges, then I will bring all of this to the Board of Education and your son will certainly be suspended for his actions last week. Additionally, I am sure the local news will have a field day spreading the juicy gossip all over the place about your son and the corruption that you tried to enforce. Am I clear?"

Ted sat in silence for a moment letting what Roger said sink in.

"That also sounds like blackmail, Principal," said Ted.

"You're damn right it is, Ted. Enough is enough. I'm not proud of it but there's no alternative with you."

"What about Jason and Lori?" asked Debbie.

"I'll get to them in a second." Then, looking back at Ted, said, "So, what do you say Ted?"

Ted realized that Roger had managed to back him into a corner, especially with the threat of going to the press. He then said, "I have one question."

"What's that?"

"Why did you decide to record the conversation?"

Roger put his phone back in his pocket and said, "Because I had a feeling that Jason was innocent even though I was tough on him. Jason doesn't do things like cheat and vandalize cars. Because I've let you push me around too much in just a few months and I've had enough. I didn't know about the headsets until this afternoon when Lori stopped in, and I wasn't going to sit by while their reputations were compromised by a bully buying his way out of his son's bad behavior. So, for the last time, do you agree?"

Ted stared at Roger for a moment, secretly impressed, and replied, "Yes."

"Good," said Roger. He swiveled to face all four parents and continued, "Now, here's what we're going to do about Trevor, Jason, and Lori ..."

IV.

Epilogue

32.

It could have been much worse.

Trevor, Jason, and Lori stayed after school for three straight weeks to help the custodial staff clean the high school after hours. They also had to wash every teacher's car and since they could not wash all the cars at once, they were also responsible for coming up with a schedule, so that each teacher could make an individual appointment. This schedule needed to include alternate dates in case of rain or other potential conflicts.

Jason and Lori didn't mind working together but the real punishment was working with Trevor the whole time. The first week was pretty miserable, but then they all seemed to get along better by the second and third week. They weren't becoming friends anytime soon, but there was a mutual understanding that there was no way out of the punishment; they needed to work well together to avoid having the punishment extended. Mr. Hagen made that point very clear.

Jason got his phone back and was no longer grounded. John, Debbie, and Paula were never going to be okay with what their kids did at Southfield's; however, Jason and Lori's determination to clear Jason's name was commendable, and they really couldn't fault them fully for their actions. Still, they were glad it was all over with and Ted got his equipment back without any drama. Also, they all agreed that the school punishment was fair enough and didn't add to it at home.

Steve and Pete kept their jobs at Southfield's and Benny, Trevor's look-out man, spent a week afterschool with Mrs. Goldfeather, helping her clean the entire classroom, especially the grimy, biology lab.

33.

THE DAY AFTER THE MONDAY NIGHT MEETING, JANE STAFFORD WENT INTO Ted's office to discuss another matter with him. She looked ashen and pale as she sat down across from him.

"Are you all right, Jane?" asked Ted with genuine concern.

"To be honest, not really," replied Jane, looking down at her hands.

"What is it?"

She raised her head and looked at Ted. "I have an update on the Red Chip and user manual."

Ted smiled softly. "I handed them over last night. Everything's fine."

Jane shook her head. "There *were*, in fact, two Red Chips originally in that envelope, but we have only gotten one back."

Ted, sitting up straighter and fighting like hell to keep his emotions in check, responded, "I don't understand. Are you sure?"

"Yes, I'm sure. I called Steve this morning and he assured me that he only had one Red Chip and one user manual. I believe him, Ted. You remember how he was at the meeting."

Ted's desk phone buzzed, which was rare.

The nervous voice on the other end said, "Excuse me, Mr. Collins?"

"Yes, what is it?" said Ted, shaking his head while looking at Jane.

"This is Bob from the front desk. There are some people here to see you."

"I'm a little busy, Bob. Tell them to call and make an appointment."

"I don't think that's going to be possible." Bob now had a Taser jammed into his neck.

"Bob, I'm hanging up now."

"S ... S ... Samantha Morrison."

The line went dead. Ted stared at Jane for a moment, swallowed hard, and then said, "Jane, listen to me. You need to leave the building through the side door *right now.*"

"What's going on, Ted?"

"I have no time to explain it, but let's just say that this technology means more to the people who just showed up in our lobby than anything else on this planet."

"Why are they here?"

"I have no idea. I gave them what they needed. You seriously need to get out of here."

Ted and Jane stood and just as Jane reached the door, Ted called out, "Wait. You didn't finish your update. Quickly, where's the other Red Chip now?"

"We don't know."

34.

Valhalla

WANDA PLATTS, THE DEPUTY DIRECTOR OF NATIONAL INTELLIGENCE, was secretly thrilled to be at the facility, putting the screws to Nicolas for his error. Ever since she left his living room, after he first arrived at his new home three years ago, she has been patiently waiting for her chance to nail him.

"Nicolas, help me understand how not one, but two chips have gotten out of your possession and into the hands of these kids," said Wanda.

Nicolas, Wanda, and Christoph, Wanda's aide, were staring up at the big screen at another teenager's school I.D. Nicolas was visibly irritated, not only because there was a new, rogue chip floating around, but because he now needed to explain again what he had already told these people over the phone.

"Wanda, we never had possession of these chips. We were originally told that we had all of the prototypes and had no reason not to believe the gentleman who dropped them off."

"You know, for someone as arrogant as you, you seemed to have been easily played by someone not nearly as bright as you. And, if that wasn't bad enough, now high school kids are finding out about this new technology that could jeopardize everything we've built up to this point. You do understand that if this project fails, the United States Government may not be willing to extend this generous gift to you and your family and you may find yourself out in a Colorado cage after all."

Nicolas continued to stare at the screen, unwilling to make eye contact. He was furious about so many things, including this cheap attack by his own government for something that was out of his control.

Wanda continued, "It could take weeks to formulate a plan to question these kids; an eternity as far as this operation goes."

"Any type of a delay is risky and dangerous," replied Nicolas.

"Well, this is the situation you've put us in," snapped Wanda, really testing Nicolas's patience now.

Nicolas stood up straight and looked at Wanda. "Look Wanda. Let's cut the crap. We can fix this mess right now, and yet you're standing here giving me a lecture about losing time because of protocols." Nicolas then tapped the employee at the computer console on the shoulder and said, "Print the address out for me."

"Yes, sir."

"Where are you going?" asked Wanda.

"My office. I need to make a call. There may be a faster way to nip this in the bud. Bear with me for ten minutes or so."

"Make it quick."

Nicolas walked toward his office but ducked into the conference room where the two visitors dropped their bags and coats when they arrived. He knew enough that continuing to argue with Wanda would be a complete waste of time and energy and decided right then to take matters into his own hands. Nicolas didn't feel like rolling the dice to find out if the government was bluffing about reneging on their arrangement.

He grabbed the set of car keys that sat on the table and placed them in his pocket. He then walked out of the conference room and into the back stairwell that Ted was escorted up a few months earlier. Nicolas emerged in the lobby and then walked out to the front of the building, unlocked the door of the black Cadillac, got into the car, and started it. He realized two things at that very moment: he didn't have a driver's license and he hadn't been behind the wheel of a car in years. He adjusted the mirrors, put the car in drive, and pulled away.

There was one last obstacle to get through in the form of a fiberglass gate at the guardhouse leading out of the back of the facility. As it came into view, he saw the guard stand up in the guardhouse and instead of attempting to explain the situation, for which the guard would most certainly not let him pass, he applied additional pressure to the accelerator. When the guard saw the car speeding toward him, he dove back into the guardhouse moments before Nicolas barreled through the gate, shattering it to pieces and continuing out of the property.

The guard scrambled to his feet and called into the facility to alert his boss as to what happened.

"This is Guardhouse B. I can't swear to it, but I'm pretty sure I just saw Mr. Foster drive out of the back gate." The guard listened to the response and then replied, "A black Cadillac and I didn't catch the license plate." Another pause and then, "Yes, he's gone. The gate is completely shattered."

The guard on the other end of the call rose out of her seat and walked into the main Lab and approached Wanda and Christoph.

"Ma'am, we have a situation."

"What is it?" replied Wanda, now looking around.

"We believe Nicolas has left the premises."

"What? He was just here a moment ago. He knows he can't leave."

"Ma'am, I understand but I have to ask for your full attention here. Your black Cadillac was just used to drive through our back gate."

Christoph now turned to face the guard and instinctively felt his front two pockets for his car keys and realized that he did not possess them.

"Get us a car, now," said Wanda. "I don't care whose it is but we need it out front in three minutes."

"Yes, ma'am." The guard turned and ran back out of the lab.

Wanda turned to Christoph and said, "Grab your things and pull up the tracker for the car on your phone. Let's try to mop up this mess before alerting anyone else."

"We need to call this in," said Christoph.

"*I* need to call it in, and we'll do it when I say so. Let's go."

Wanda and Christoph quickly walked out of the lab to attempt to track down Nicolas before the situation got completely out of hand.

Back in the Cadillac, driving along I-78, Nicolas removed the print out from his back pocket and pulled up the car's GPS on the dashboard. The car's computer would not allow him to input the address while the car was moving, so Nicolas pulled off onto the shoulder and brought the car to a full stop. It took him a few minutes to figure out the system but he managed to type in the address properly. After a moment, the GPS alerted him that he was thirty-five minutes away.

As he pulled off the shoulder and back into the right lane, he thought more about the absurdity of the whole situation but also knew that three years' worth of work was not going to come to a crashing halt because of a few high school kids. Nicolas got the Cadillac up to eighty miles per hour as he closed in on his target.

35.

The Night Before

AFTER RETRIEVING THE SMALL, BLACK BOX—THE SAME ONE HE POCKETED days earlier at Southfield's—from his desk drawer, he snapped the Red Chip into place and entered in the last few pieces of information from the photocopied user manual into the program. He then pressed Enter and placed the headset, that he also took the night of the fire, over his face. As the countdown clock reached "1" and the black screen separated, Pete's mouth slowly opened. He could not believe what he was seeing.

To Be
Continued

ACKNOWLEDGEMENTS

Writing anything for the public is hard. Writing a novel, without any support, is all but impossible. I'd like to recognize a few people who went above and beyond in helping me get this book to the finish line.

Thank you to...

Chris Perez, a good friend and fellow writer, who has been supportive of this book from day one. There are only a couple of people who I will bounce ideas off of and allow to read my messy drafts. Chris is one of those people.

Bradley Heller, who has been, and continues to be, a constant support with this, and other projects. Your encouragement is critical.

Charity Hertzog, one of my oldest friends, who provided great feedback on this book as well as my three children's books.

Cara Strickler who managed to find the sneakiest errors as well as correct some really awful sentences.

Jennifer Brown, who offered great comments, as well as hours of conversation on this, and many other topics.

Jessica, who read this story before anyone, when it was half-baked, and encouraged me to head in this new direction.

Jordan Eagles whose edits, comments, suggestions, and questions proved vital to getting this story to a good place.

Anita Carroll for designing an amazing cover.

My mom, aunt, and sister, for their support and for reading an early version.

My cat, Stella, for the daily reminders to eat, play, and sleep.

Many additional friends of mine whose words of encouragement and general interest in this book, among other ventures, continues to keep me motivated.

My fellow writers and book people on *Instagram*. Your honest updates and thoughts are incredibly encouraging, inspiring, and important.

And, last but not least, YOU. Thank you, Reader, for taking the time. I hope you enjoyed yourself.

IF YOU LIKED THIS BOOK...

Please help other readers easily find it by leaving a review on *Amazon* or *Goodreads*. Thank you so much.

www.amazon.com/author/jeffmagnuson

Jeff Magnuson is the author of three children's books, including the multi-award-winning *Charley's Cat Family*. He earned his MBA from the University of North Carolina at Chapel Hill and is now a full-time writer and career coach living in northern New Jersey. *Don't Look Back* is his first novel. You can connect with him on Instagram (@jeffmagnusonwrites) and at **www.jeffmagnusonwrites.com**.

Made in the USA
Middletown, DE
13 December 2020

27591659R00129

Jason Markum is an ordinary high school sophomore facing a suspension after getting blamed by the class bully.

Ted Collins is a wealthy technology developer whose greed is about to catch up with him as he completes a new project for a secret government group.

When part of this project—technology that's never been seen before, in the form of a circular, red computer chip—finds its way into the hands of Jason and his friend, Lori, they soon discover an alarming new world.

The secrets in their possession have a greater power than anyone can imagine and Jason and Lori will need to act quickly if they are going to get him off the hook at school or both face consequences far worse than a suspension.

ISBN 9780999098264

9 780999 098264